DEMON
DESIGN

ALSO BY
M.J. HAAG

FAIRY TALE RETELLINGS
(ALL IN THE SAME WORLD)

BEASTLY TALES

Depravity

Deceit

Devastation

TALES OF CINDER

Disowned (prequel)

Defiant

Disdain

Damnation

RESURRECTION CHRONICLES
(hottie demons!)

Demon Ember	*Demon Escape*	*Demon Dawn*
Demon Flames	*Demon Deception*	*Dmeon Disgrace*
Demon Ash	*Demon Night*	*Demon Fall*

DEMON DESIGN

A RESURRECTION CHRONICLES NOVELLA

M.J. HAAG

Shattered Glass
— PUBLISHING —

To the hope of summer after a really long winter.

WHAT HAS HAPPENED BEFORE...

After thousands of years trapped in their underground prison, the dark fey, with their grey skin and reptilian eyes, have emerged. They alone can kill the hellhounds and help bring a stop to the plague unleashed by the earthquakes. They only ask for one thing in return: a chance to meet women who might love them as they are.

CHAPTER ONE

"ARE YOU EVER GOING TO GO TO SLEEP, BROOKE?" SAM GRUMBLED from the top bunk.

"Give me another minute," I said softly from my chair near the window.

The pencil slipped from my numb fingers and clattered to the floor. If my other housemates had heard the noise, they were too tired and cold to complain. I winced at the sound regardless, thinking of the damage I'd caused the soft lead. There were no more cans of beans to trade for another even if there were more pencils in this place.

After inspecting the tip, I returned to my sketch in progress of Tenacity's lit up perimeter wall. No matter how many times I looked at the thing, I marveled at its ingenuity. Cars, once prized possessions and now dangerous and pointless noisemakers, stood tailpipe to headlight around the subdivision. Smaller vehicles and bits of other metal things filled in any gaps. The protective barrier wasn't pretty, but it was very much a work of art. I added some shading to a car handle then flipped back the pages until I found the ones from a few weeks ago.

The sketch of a heavily muscled man with long hair and pointed ears looked like a fantasy depiction of an elf. But it wasn't. The existence of the dark fey was our reality now, spawned into existence by earthquakes and plague. I studied his strong jawline and angular cheekbones. He was the true work of art. Yes, his looks fascinated me. But so did many other traits.

One of the few human volunteers, I was here when they'd built the wall. I'd marveled at their strength as they lifted and moved the cars into place. Their agility as they jumped almost twenty feet into the air. Their easy-going and curious attitudes toward us when they received nothing but hate in return. Except for that one group of men who tried to steal some women. I didn't even feel a little bad about how they met their end.

I continued to flip through the pages, looking at the one particular fey who'd caught my eye while they'd been here. There was something about him that wouldn't leave me alone. Because of that, there were dozens of sketches of him. Most I'd drawn from memory.

Standing with a stretch, I set my sketch pad and pencil on the chair seat then crawled under my covers without taking off any of my clothes. At some point in the middle of the night, I'd be warm enough to take my jacket off, but I wasn't there yet.

"God, I wish they would just throw more wood in the stove," Sam said when her teeth started to chatter.

"Unless you're willing to go chop some wood, that's not going to happen."

The fey had been good to make sure that there were enough

solar panels and wood stoves for all of the houses. The solar panels and the battery banks were enough to keep the lights on for a while and run a few space heaters, which kept the house at a steady fifty-five degrees Fahrenheit. We weren't freezing, but we weren't exactly warm either.

The wood stove could have been a solution if there was more firewood. Our house wasn't the only one economically doling out firewood to the stove. We had our weekly allotment from the firewood pile the fey had made while they were still here, but it was never enough. There was always the option of going out and cutting some more ourselves, but everyone was too afraid to leave the perimeter wall to get what they needed. If the people here wouldn't have been such asshats to the fey, they would still be helping us rather than leaving us on our own.

Sighing, I curled into a ball and thought about the choices that had brought me here. At the time I'd volunteered to join the work crew building the wall around Tenacity, I'd thought I was so smart. It hadn't been easy. I'd spent a lot of cold nights with the other humans in the temporary house. But I thought it would be worth it to scope out the houses and have first pick. Unfortunately, that wasn't how it worked. Matt Davis kept things "fair" in that he assigned houses via a random drawing.

If I hadn't been here working, I would have been in Tolerance the day the infected breached their walls. That was where Matt and Mya, the current leader of a select group of humans and the fey, had stuck the survivors from Whiteman's military base. Those assholes had ruined it for everyone with their anti-fey attitudes. Instead of welcoming anyone to the settlement, only a select few were invited to stay. Women, mostly, since that's what they fey were lacking. But a few families who were nice got to stay too.

While I shivered at the thought of having to run for my life again from those plague-ravaged humans, part of me wished I would have been there instead of here. There was nothing here but a constant struggle for survival, a slow starvation, and a growing bitterness.

I hadn't given up hope of living in Tolerance, though. And I think a few ladies from Tolerance hadn't given up on the people here in Tenacity either, based on their invitations to teach the fey social skills. A grin tugged at my lips as I thought of the dinner dates they were hard-selling to the single ladies. They were smart; I'd give them that. A hot meal and sleeping in a house with heat was tempting. But I knew what the dates were for and didn't want to get some fey's hopes up. Not when I kept dreaming of one fey in particular.

Each morning, a crew of fey would show up from Tolerance to recruit Tenacity volunteers for a supply run. Not that there were ever very many willing to go on the dangerous gathering missions. There were too many risks and too few rewards to motivate people. No one was allowed to keep everything they gathered. The fey received the majority, since they did all the hard work, while Tenacity kept the rest to split up as Matt saw fit. The volunteers who went out only kept a small percentage of what they gathered. But even having a little more than anyone else in this place put a target on your back. So, people starved, and I stood in the group outside the gates and watched for the fey I sketched.

Either I kept missing him, or he wasn't one of the regulars who went out for a supply run. I wished I would have had the courage to flag him down and ask him his name when we were still working on the wall together. But he and the rest of the fey had been so terrifyingly new then. Not anymore, though.

Desperation was a raw and irrational thing. The near kidnapping of those girls a few weeks ago showed Tenacity already had the disease, and I needed out before it sunk its teeth into me.

I needed to find my sketch-fey soon.

CHAPTER TWO

I STOOD AT THE GATE, ONE OF THE FEW PEOPLE WAITING FOR THE fey, at first light. And, just like every other morning, the fey from my sketchbook didn't show up. That was okay, though. I had a Plan B and spotted her familiar face across the distance. Emily wasn't very popular with some folks in Tenacity, but she was smart and always showed up with a fey escort.

Last night, while shivering in bed and waiting to pass out, I'd decided I was done waiting and hoping my sketch-fey would turn up. It was time to take some action. And Plan B had been born.

I hurried toward Emily as Matt called out for any volunteers from Tenacity who'd like to join the fey on a supply run.

"Hey, Emily. Do you have a second?" I asked.

She looked up from her sheet of paper and smiled at me.

"Brooke, right?" she asked.

"Right."

"How can I help you? Are you interested in signing up for a dinner date?"

My guilty gaze shifted to the fey beside her. The fey were a little hard to read sometimes because they didn't have expressive faces. That, or they chose not to express themselves facially. Regardless, I knew what answer he was probably hoping for. It was the whole reason all the fey kept showing up.

"I'm sorry. No. I was wondering if you could talk to Mya on my behalf."

"About what?"

I opened the sketch pad I'd brought with me, just in case, and opened it to my drawing of the wall.

"I haven't seen Tolerance," I explained. "I was here, helping with the wall. But I'd really like to visit and do some sketches."

"I think I can safely answer on Mya's behalf with permission for a day trip so you can get some inspiration. Tor would be more than willing to take you over there now if you'd like."

I glanced at the huge fey then Emily.

"That would be great, but I don't want to leave you walking around town alone. Not everyone is happy about the dinners."

She smiled at me. "I was planning on talking to Matt anyway. Tor can be back before I'm finished. Right, Tor?"

The fey gave a single nod before focusing on me.

"Can I carry you?" he asked, his voice a smooth rumble.

"Sure. Thank you."

Emily beamed at me and waved as Tor scooped me up and took off at a run. This wasn't my first fey ride. I knew to hide my face from the wind and avoid as much touching as possible.

It didn't take him long to reach Tolerance's walls. When he set me down safely inside, I looked around.

"Do I need to let anyone know that I'm here?" I asked.

"Drav is in there, looking for chocolate," Tor said, pointing at the nearest house. "Talk to him."

"Thanks."

Tor nodded and pivoted before running up the wall. I stared

after him for a moment, completely mesmerized by that agile display, before hurrying toward the house he'd indicated. Someone had posted a sign on the door that said, "Take what you need but don't get greedy. Only leave with one box of ziti."

I knocked as I read the sign and nearly peed myself when an angry looking fey jerked the door open a second later.

"Drav?" I asked nervously. "Tor said I should talk to you."

"Good. Help me find something chocolate."

He turned and walked away from the door, not waiting for my reply. Without him blocking the view, I saw what this house was being used for. Shelving units crowded the once open space of the living room, creating rows of food supplies.

Drav paced to the end of the main aisle and looked back at me. His body language screamed impatience, so I hurried forward.

"What type of chocolate are you looking for?" I asked.

"Any type."

I plucked a box of brownie mix off the shelf.

"This is a chocolate dessert called brownies. It's a box mix." I turned it over to look at the back. "To make it correctly, you need eggs, oil, and water. But you can just add a little water and eat it like that, too, and it'll still be good."

"Thank you." He took the box from me and started for the door.

"Um, Drav? Tor said that I should talk to you about spending the day here. I only want to draw. I promise not to cause any trouble."

He grunted and left without a backward glance.

Alone in Tolerance's supply house, I looked around at all of the food. Our supply shed had a few totes of random-ass food that Matt doled out with caution. The sad quantity was because most of the food came here. I knew that lack of sharing was

Matt and Mya's doing and not the fey, though. And I couldn't blame the stance of the two leaders when almost no one from Tenacity went on the supply runs. The people there hated the fey, treated them like shit, but expected handouts. I wouldn't give Tenacity any of this food either.

My stomach let out a loud growl. It wasn't easy to walk out the door without taking anything. But I'd heard raiding the supply house was what had severely damaged the relationship between the people of Tolerance and those now in Tenacity. I didn't want to continue the animosity.

Outside of the house, I stopped a moment to get my bearings. Like Tenacity, Tolerance wasn't a small subdivision, and the wall stretched farther than I could see. I flipped to a new page in my sketchbook and started creating a rough map of the town. It gave me a reason to wander and to ask about who lived where.

It didn't take long for me to notice the biggest difference between this town and the other. The fey were everywhere here. I didn't spot them at first because they were good at blending in with their surroundings. But once I spotted them, I couldn't unsee how many there were.

All without a woman of their own.

All watching me with far too much focus.

As much as I wanted to keep my head down and carry on with little interaction, I knew I couldn't do that. I was there for a specific reason.

"Hello," a deep voice said behind me. "My name is Turik. What is your name?"

With a friendly smile on my lips, I turned to the fey. He wasn't my sketch-fey, but maybe he could help me.

"I'm Brooke. Can you tell me if you know this fey?" I asked, turning the page to the one I had marked.

The fey glanced at the sketch before his intense regard returned to my face. I was about to ask again when he finally answered.

"I know him."

"Great. What's his name? Can you tell me where to find him?"

"His name is Solin. He is in the house with the red shutters. Would you like me to carry you there?"

"What? No, thanks. I can manage." I hurried away, eager to escape the unwanted help.

Each fey I passed as I searched nodded to me in greeting. I smiled back but didn't slow down. Now that I was here, I didn't want to waste any time. I had a fey to talk to. While I walked, I considered what I'd say.

Oh, wow! A familiar face. You probably don't remember me, but we worked together on the wall over in Tenacity. My name's Brooke. It's good to see you again.

It was a decent, friendly opening. Enough to get me invited inside, hopefully.

The house was two blocks over. Nerves danced in my stomach as I studied the house. Now that I was there, I wasn't sure what to do next. I knew what to say, but it wouldn't work if I just walked right up to his door and knocked. Shit. What excuse did I have for knocking? Bathroom. Yeah, I'll ask to use his bathroom because I was here sketching. Perfect.

I looked down at my pad and wondered if I should sketch his house or something first.

"What kind of book is that?" a fey asked, distracting me.

"Oh, it's a—"

The words died as I tilted my head back and looked up into familiar, bright green eyes.

CHAPTER THREE

THE WORDS I'D WANTED TO SAY EVAPORATED, AND ALL I COULD DO was stare up at him as he waited patiently for an answer I couldn't form. Towering over me by more than a foot, he was so much more intimidating than I remembered.

I blinked at him stupidly, soaking up the details of features I'd sketched so often. Dear Lord, was that a cleft in his chin? How had I missed that?

My tongue-tied state lasted all of three seconds before words started pouring out.

"It's a sketchbook. For drawing. With my pencil." I held up the treasured implement like a toddler, realized how ridiculous I looked, and quickly put it down.

"I make drawings of the things I see. Sometimes, it's just because I like what I see and want to remember it. You know, since there's no internet anymore or corner drug stores to develop photos the old way. I've done a few commissioned pieces. One of the married ladies in Tenacity traded me a can of corn to do a sketch of her. She wanted to give it to her husband for their anniversary. Personally, I think he would have rather had the corn, but her heart was in the right place."

"Show me."

"The corn? I already ate it."

He blinked at me.

"Can I see your drawings?" he asked.

I wanted to smack my forehead.

"Oh, yeah. Sure. Sorry. Of course, you meant the sketches and not the corn." I gave a nervous laugh and quickly opened the book to my sketch of Sam. It was a quick one I'd done of her while she was sleeping.

He grunted as he took the sketch pad from me and studied the artwork.

"I'm here to look around and sketch a little. Drav gave me permission. I think. He was kind of busy looking for chocolate in the storage house. I didn't take anything."

Sketch-fey grunted again and turned the page. Thankfully, the next one was of Tenacity's perimeter wall and not of him. However, the way he looked at me and pinned me with his intense green gaze made me nervous. Maybe he remembered me now? Shit. This was where I was supposed to introduce myself.

"It's Brooke. I mean, my name's Brooke. You probably remember that wall. You built it with the cars, right?" I closed my mouth and fought the overwhelming urge to open it again. Why couldn't I just shut up already?

"You want to remember the cars?"

"No, I sketched the wall because I find it interesting. It's like art. I figure maybe someone will want to hang it on their wall or something since there are a lot of bare walls in the houses."

"You give your sketches away?"

"Some of them. If people are interested in what I draw."

He looked at me speculatively.

"Is there something you want me to sketch for you?"

"Yes. Me."

I'd died and gone to heaven. It didn't matter that it was cold outside and my feet were freezing. My face ignited with heat.

"Okay. Sure. Yeah. I can do that." I forced myself to stop and breathe. The silence grew as he continued to watch me expectantly. Problem was I had no clue what he wanted from me. "Um, do you want me to come back later, or do you have time now?"

"I have time now."

He started toward the house with the red shutters, and my pulse leapt again as I realized what was happening. He was inviting me inside. To make a sketch of him. My mystery-fey.

"Uh, you haven't told me your name," I said as I hurried to keep up.

He paused and looked back at me.

"Solin."

I smiled. "It's nice to finally meet you, Solin."

He blinked at me, and I realized what I'd said.

"I saw you when we were building Tenacity's wall."

He studied me for a moment like I was the first human he'd ever seen. Then, he opened the door. I smiled to myself and hurried after him. Heat lovingly wrapped around me the moment we went inside. I basked in it and slowly removed my gloves and hat. A second later, the smell hit me.

"Is that pancakes?" I asked.

He grunted and walked farther into the house, passing the wall that partitioned the entry from the rest of the house.

"Hey, Solin," a female voice called. "I hope you're hungry. I made a double batch of spam to go with these cakes."

With a sinking feeling in my stomach, I woodenly followed in his steps and saw a beautiful blonde at the kitchen stove.

"Hi," I said weakly, recognizing Sophia from my time in the Whiteman camp.

"Hey, Brooke. How ya doing?" Her welcoming smile disappeared as she looked at me. "Actually, I can see you're not well. Is something wrong?"

Everything was wrong. Not for one second had I even considered that he might have already hooked up with someone. I felt sick to my stomach and just wanted to go home and curl into a ball. God, I'd already made such an ass of myself. I refused to make it worse by crying and running from the house like some teenage drama queen. I would salvage what I could of the situation.

"It's the food," I said weakly. "I haven't eaten yet today, and I think the smell just got to me."

Sophia's expression turned sympathetic.

"I'm glad Solin invited you in for breakfast. Come sit down."

Solin slowly turned his head to look at me like I was the devil come to roost. He probably wanted me to draw and leave. Given the turn of events, most girls would probably do just that. But I didn't care if my hopes were shattered at my feet. I'd walk through the shards for a chance at an actual meal.

"Thank you."

I set my sketch pad on the counter and accepted the plate she handed to me.

"How are things at Tenacity? Still a bunch of assholes making each other even more miserable?"

"Pretty much. Had I known I'd end up on the wrong side of the tracks when I signed up to help with the wall, I would have reconsidered."

Solin stared hard at me for a moment. I couldn't tell if he was still trying to place me or wishing I'd shut up.

"It's not too late," Sophia said. "I could talk to Mya for you. Or you could just sign up for one of the dinner dates. Any fey would be willing to take you in like Solin did for me."

She smiled at Solin, and the tips of his ears turned a dark grey. He looked down at his plate like the attention embarrassed him. Ugh, why was he so adorable?

"Thanks, but I think I'll pass for now."

Sophia didn't make a big deal about it and turned the conversation to everything that had been happening at Tolerance since she'd been there. She had a lot of questions about the almost kidnapping that had happened at Tenacity too.

Our information trade was cut short, though, when I took my last bite.

"We must go," Solin said, standing.

Sophia's brows shot up. "Okay. Should I make lunch for you two?"

He looked at me.

Despite having never considered that he might have already hooked up with a girl, I wasn't slow. I understood he was asking me how long the drawing would take. I also understood that dragging the drawing out would see me fed until it was finished.

"Yes, please," I said, not even feeling a smidge of guilt.

Solin grunted and started walking away.

"I think that means you should follow him," Sophia said with a smirk.

"Oh." I grabbed my things. "Thanks."

"Don't worry. You'll get used to it."

I hurried after Solin, catching up to him on the steps that led upstairs. The room he entered had little in it. A comfortable-looking chair and a dresser. That was it. Probably because he was sharing the master with Sophia. Yet, in the nearly empty closet, I saw two man-sized white t-shirts.

As soon as I moved past the door, Solin closed it and watched me expectantly.

"Uh. Okay. So what kind of drawing of yourself would you like?"

"I don't know."

"Maybe you can tell me what the drawing's for."

"I want Sophia to remember me when I'm gone."

"Okay. So, like a friendly drawing? A romantic one? Or maybe an erotic one?" I couldn't help myself. I had to ask because I had to know what kind of relationship he had with her.

"Yes. An erotic picture. I want her to have sex thoughts when she looks at the drawing of me."

CHAPTER FOUR

I COULDN'T BREATHE. IT PROBABLY HAD SOMETHING TO DO WITH the way my heart was hammering and the way my chest felt like it had a boulder on it.

He folded his arms, a simple move for any mortal man, but Solin didn't fit that category. The way his biceps bulged and how his shirt pulled tight across his chest made him a Greek god, chiseled from marble.

"How do you draw an erotic picture?" he asked, interrupting my daydream of petting marble.

"It's hot in here, right?" After shedding the jacket, I fanned myself with the sketch pad for a moment.

He watched me and continued to wait for an answer. What in the hell had I gotten myself into?

"Well, um, first you'll need to undress," I rasped.

He immediately tugged off his shirt, exposing a gloriously ridged abdomen and chiseled pectorals. A small sound escaped me. Maybe a whimper. I couldn't be sure because my blood was pounding too loudly in my ears.

Solin heard, though, and paused with his hands on his pants to look up at me.

"Keep going," I managed. "I'm fine."

He grunted and whisked his pants off in a blink. I couldn't look away from the thick shaft that hung between his legs.

My pencil clattered to the floor. It took a moment for the sound to register and for me to realize I was standing there gawking. Shaking my shock, I bent down to retrieve what I'd dropped. However, while bent down, I looked up again. *It* was eye level, and I couldn't look away. There was this really large vein that ran along the underside, twisting around to the top.

"What should I do next?" he asked.

I swallowed hard and managed to tear my gaze away from his junk. The look he was giving me when I finally straightened spoke volumes. I had to be seven shades of crazy in his mind.

"Uh, well, I guess you need to decide what you want this picture to say about you. It'll help me know how to position you." My gaze flicked down to his dick, and I flushed scarlet. "I mean, like, do you want her to see you as a smart guy because then I could pose you in a chair and have you reading a book."

"I can't read."

"Right. I remember that about you. I mean all fey. It's really cool how fast you picked up our spoken language, though."

He grunted.

"So back to how you want Sophia to see you?"

He considered me for a moment.

"I want her to see that I am ready to taste her pussy."

"Uh. Okay." I could already picture him on his back, holding his own cock as he stroked himself while he thought of tasting me. I meant her. Sophia. I fanned myself again. *Dear Lord, save me from my own dumb ideas.*

"Let's start with a simple pose for practice, and we'll work up to the pussy-tasting heat level."

"Show me this simple pose."

I eased myself down to the carpet and lay on my back with my hands behind my head and one knee bent.

"Like this," I said.

He nodded, and I scurried out of the way. With my back to him, I opened the blinds to let natural light in. When I turned around, I forgot my own name.

Solin lay just as I'd indicated, arms behind his head and one knee slightly bent. Mid-morning light warmed his grey skin, making every one of his sun-kissed ab-ridges stand out. His biceps looked perfectly biteable. And his legs. The cords of muscle on his thick thighs begged for exploring.

There was just one thing off. That beautiful length of made-for-her-pleasure between his legs needed to hang to the right, draped over his thigh to show just how magnificently long he was.

I didn't consciously think, *hey, I should move his boy bits around.* I just did it. And I was mid-nut-fluff before I realized I was plumping his testicles. I jerked my hands back.

"Sorry!" I jumped to my feet and fumbled for my sketch pad.

The few minutes I needed to flip to the next open page weren't nearly enough to calm the raging storm of embarrassment inside of me. So, I took my time and made a show out of checking my pencil and doing a few side shadings to test the tip.

When my face felt slightly less on fire, I sat on the floor and got to work. I couldn't look him in the eye. Or the groin. So I focused on the general pose, using lines to get the angles right and slowly adding the details.

I was so caught up in what I was doing that I startled when Sophia called from below that lunch was ready.

Solin gracefully rose to his feet and grabbed his pants, unconcerned with the fact he was dressing in front of me. I pretended to study my sketch until he strode out the door and I could vigorously fan myself unobserved.

Breathing calmed, I went downstairs. Both Sophia and Solin were already at the table, waiting for me.

"Would you mind if I used a bathroom first? I'll be quick if you point me in the right direction."

Sophia gave Solin a censuring look. "You didn't show her around?"

His gaze shifted between the two of us, and I could tell he was confused.

"It's okay," I said.

Sophia made a noise that said it wasn't then took me on a quick tour of their house. There were two full bathrooms stocked with toiletries, a guest half bath, four bedrooms, and a fully finished basement with a pool table and an old pinball machine. I was so jealous of their house. The one I was staying in was better than the tent that had been assigned to me at Whiteman, but nowhere near as nice as this place.

After I used the guest bathroom, I rejoined them. Once again, Sophia directed the conversation around the two of us, and I began to wonder if she was just trying to include me or if she maybe knew Solin wasn't the talkative type. After all, I'd spent hours in that room with him, and he'd barely spoken.

When we finished eating, I thanked Sophia for lunch, and Solin and I returned to the sketch room. Without prompting, Solin stripped and resumed his position on the floor. Only, it was a bit off from the first position. His hair was tucked under his head this time, not streaming out behind him as it had before. And his dick was once again hiding. Since I'd avoided that part during the first round, I really needed it out again.

"Can you rearrange yourself like I did?" I asked, my voice a strained rasp.

"I don't understand."

My face heated, and I waved a hand toward his groin. He glanced down then reached for his sack, plumping it up like I had.

"Like this?"

I opened my mouth, but no words came out. I'd been struck dumb by the sight of him playing with himself. Even shaking my head took effort.

"You do it," he said, folding his arms behind his head again.

My palms grew sweaty as I knelt beside him. To help calm my racing heart, I arranged his hair first. The silky strands ran through my fingers, and I may have played with them more than necessary. I may have also used the task as an excuse to "accidentally" run my fingers over his arms. His muscles twitched under my touch, but he didn't comment.

Not your man, I started chanting in my head to keep myself on track.

When I finished, I shifted my focus to the magic-maker innocently napping between his thighs. Knowing I needed to be more professional and less gropey about this, I tried to use two fingers to reposition it. Somehow, two fingers turned into two hands and some brief vein exploration.

"Like that," I croaked. Turning away from him, I wiped my trembling palms over my stomach then picked up my supplies.

He watched me as I sat. Once again, my muteness broke, and words came pouring out.

"Sorry about being so handsy. It helps to keep the position the same so the perspective stays consistent. That's why I'm sitting in the same spot. I hope it didn't make you feel uncomfortable. All part of the drawing process. So, tell me about Sophia."

He blinked at me, probably stunned by the word vomit I'd just spewed his way.

"You do not know her?" he asked.

"I've met her, but I probably don't know her like you do. What's her favorite color?"

He frowned slightly, an intimidating look on any of his kind.

"I do not know."

"Okay. How about her favorite food?"

"She likes all food."

I glanced from his crotch on the paper to his real-life face.

"Sure. Given the state of supplies, we're grateful for what we can get. But what about her favorite food before the world broke?"

"She said she likes all food," he reiterated.

"Bullshit. We all have a favorite."

"What's yours?"

"Mac and cheese with chopped pickles topped with a buttery tortilla chip crumble."

He blinked at me.

"Don't judge. It's fantastic."

"It's not a food I've heard of. What's your favorite color?"

"That depends on the day and my mood. Most days, I like red. Some days, I lean more toward green. I'm looking forward to summer and seeing trees and life again. But winter can be pretty too in its own way. Well, it usually is. It's been a little hard to see the beauty in it this year, what with the hellhounds and the zombies and all, you know?"

He grunted and moved slightly, which shifted his dick

again. Without thinking, I leaned forward and put it back where it belonged.

"What about you?" I asked. "What's your favorite food?"

The rest of the sketch session continued with a lot of conversation, which seemed to make him restless because he shifted around a lot. I didn't mind readjusting his equipment, but all of the touching did make it a little difficult to meet Sophia's eyes when she called us to dinner. Hopefully, she would understand my sacrifice when he finally gifted her with a picture.

CHAPTER FIVE

Solin carried me home after dark along with three of his friends to make sure I was delivered safely. I tried not to focus on how great his arms felt around me or look up at his chiseled jawline or remember the way his junk had been hot and heavy in my hands. Instead, I focused on what I'd eat tomorrow.

My stomach somersaulted when he jumped over the wall and landed by the storage shed. He put me down gently. Losing the heat of his arms and all that hard muscle was a disappointment I hid well.

"Thanks for the lift home."

"It was my pleasure. May I see the picture?"

"Oh. Sure."

I glanced around to make sure the guards on the top of the wall weren't watching. Technically, they were only casting dirty looks my way. Nothing steady enough to see a naked drawing. Still, I turned slightly to flip open the pad.

The main sketch, in the middle of the paper, was his pose in all its glory. But there were other sketches around it. One of

Solin's pointed, grey ear because I'd wanted to practice all the curves and proportions apart from the main pose so I'd get it right. Then one of his face from a side view, and a second one full on. And the final one was a close-up of his lips. There was this bow to the bottom one that just demanded its own attention.

"What do you think?" I asked.

"You are very good."

"And you're a perfect model. I loved sketching you."

He was quiet for so long I tore my gaze from his sketched perfection to look at him. He blinked at me.

"Will you teach me to sketch?"

"Sure. We'll need to find you a sketch pad and a pencil like this." I held up the pencil again, this time feeling less ridiculous. "It's a special kind with a softer lead than a school pencil. But a school pencil will work too. It's just not as easy to do the shading."

He grunted and stepped back from me.

"I will return for you at dawn."

"I'll be here," I promised.

"I DON'T KNOW how you managed to find eggs, but this is amazing," I said, digging into the yellow, scrambled mess on my plate.

"I cook what Solin brings home," Sophia said. "He and his brothers can go places we humans can't to get the good stuff. I can't even tell they're made from powder. I think Ryan said that these were from one of those big outdoors centers."

Ryan, the human brother-in-law to Drav, the fey in charge

here, went with the fey on every supply run. It was one of the many sticking points when people in Tenacity reasoned it was too dangerous to go outside the walls for supply runs. If Ryan went with the fey and they kept him safe, why wouldn't they keep the rest of us humans safe? They probably would have if so many humans hadn't been dicks to them.

"Well, it's amazing," I said, offering a smile to Solin. "Thank you."

He grunted and watched me eat, already having finished his.

As soon as I was done, he stood and started for the stairs.

"Brooke and I will be doing private things in my room," he said over his shoulder. "We will eat lunch with you."

My mouth dropped open, and my shocked gaze swung to Sophia.

"He didn't...we're not..."

Sophia started laughing.

"Don't even worry about it. They have a gift when it comes to saying things as awkward as fuck. I've learned never to assume and always to ask if I need clarification. You're fine. Go work on your super-secret project. I'll see if I can find something for lunch that'll top scrambled eggs."

I hurried after Solin and caught up to him just outside the door. He paused when I grabbed his hand and looked down at me. I quickly released him.

"You can't say stuff like that," I said quietly.

"Like what?"

"What you said back there. You made it sound like we're coming up here to have sex. You could have made Sophia jealous."

"Did I?"

"No. Thankfully, she's still okay with me being here."

He grunted and opened the door. I followed him in, but my steps slowed when I saw how the room had changed. A mattress covered with blankets laid in the center of the room now, and an art desk waited in the corner by the door. Solin had even found a swivel chair. Stacks of sketch pads, paper for watercolors, canvases, pencils, watercolor pens, tubes of oil paint, brushes, and so much more piled on the floor around the desk. I ran my fingers over the surface and picked up a few of the brushes, in awe of what he'd managed to gather in such a short time.

"Where did you find—"

The words died as I turned and found him completely naked, only one step behind me.

"Is this enough to teach me when you are done?"

My answering nod was a little slow. It took that long for my brain to register the question as my eyes feasted.

"Good. Do you need more practice pose?"

I swallowed hard, and the room grew ten degrees too warm.

"No, I don't think we need more of the practice pose. Lie down like before, but this time turn your head toward me, and use one hand to touch yourself." The last few words squeezed out of my tight throat in a croak.

He got down on the mattress and assumed the practice pose.

"Show me," he said, instead of trying to do what I'd described.

And I didn't exactly mind the hands-on positioning approach. Who was I kidding? I itched to touch him again. Since he hadn't seemed to care about it yesterday, I knelt beside the mattress, greedy to get the groping started.

"If anything is uncomfortable or you don't think you'll be able to hold the pose for long, let me know. Okay?"

He grunted.

Like the previous day, I started with positioning his head and arms. The left hand went behind his head for support and to balance his overall look with the bent knee. Then, I picked up his right hand. For a moment, I forgot myself and ran my fingers over his. They were strong and long and the pads of his fingers were rough with callouses. Same with the palm of his hand. His were hands that knew the struggle of survival.

I realized what I was doing and looked up at him.

"Sorry. Just studying so I can draw you better."

He blinked at me, which I took as permission to keep going. And I really wanted to because I couldn't wait to see how he'd react to where I intended to put his hand. However, he didn't even flinch as I set it near his groin.

I stepped back to study him. His gaze tracked me.

"It's hot as heck. Mouthwatering abs I wouldn't mind hanging a sketch of on my wall, but it doesn't exactly say sex."

I froze, realizing I'd spoken my inside thoughts out loud.

"How do we make it say sex?" he asked. "Show me what to do."

The poor guy obviously had it bad for Sophia.

"Ah. Well, I think you should look like you're stroking yourself."

"Show me."

My eyes rounded. He didn't know how to jack-off? My gaze shifted from his face to that happy length of muscle between his legs. It didn't look as relaxed as it had when he'd stripped. He wasn't hard exactly, either, but it sure looked longer.

As if in a trance, I knelt by his side again and reached out to touch him. His cock jerked before I made contact, which made my pulse jump. But it didn't stop me from going the distance. I'd touched him yesterday. This was no big deal.

"Like this," I whispered, wrapping my fingers around him and stroking down once. He grew longer and harder. I gently stroked up to his thick head, marveling at the fact that he was still growing. My fingertips couldn't touch as I circled his girth and that vein I'd noticed the day before created ridges that would make a girl scream.

A clear bead of moisture appeared at the tip, signaling I'd shown him enough.

"Just like that," I said, replacing my hand with his.

When I stood back, the sight of him slowly stroking himself as he stared at me made my heart pound so erratically I couldn't breathe right. Light-headed, I nodded and sank to the floor, reaching for my pad and pencil without taking my eyes from him.

I probably could have loosely positioned him for the initial sketch, but I wasn't going to tell him that now. The room grew warmer as I drew and he stroked himself. Pre-cum gathered and dripped over his hand as we both worked. I spent an agonizingly long time capturing that detail in a small side image and then again in the main one before moving to his face.

Through it all, Solin watched me, his gaze open and alert. He was sexy as fuck, but I knew he could do better.

"Keep looking at me, but don't see me. Instead, I want you to think about Sophia. She's naked, spread open, waiting for you to taste her...pussy." I hated using that word but knew it was a fey favorite. Their holy grail was to look at the coveted crotchal-zone on a girl. I'd thrown in tasting for fun to see what'd he do.

He reacted just as I'd hoped. His gaze grew hooded, and his breathing became shallow and fast.

"Perfect," I said. "I only need a few—"

He groaned suddenly, and his release flew out of him in white ropey jets that rose in the air before landing on his chest in rapid succession.

So many ropes...

I almost osmosis orgasmed.

CHAPTER SIX

Solin continued to stroke himself in an unhurried rhythm, his hot gaze locked on me. I swallowed hard, my gaze drifting from the sheen on his skin to that lucky grey hand that gripped my favorite piece of male anatomy. How was he still hard after all of that?

"Are you guys hungry?" Sophia called.

I jolted and dropped my pencil. How long had I been staring at him? And why were my lips wet? Please tell me I hadn't been licking them while staring at him.

"Yeah," I called, my voice breaking. "We'll be down in a minute."

Solin blinked at me but didn't stop touching himself.

"Uh, why don't you go clean up and take a break? You earned it. You did great." Those last words came out a little too breathy.

His lips twitched slightly like he was going to smile, then he grabbed his shirt to clean off his chest and stood. My mouth went dry, and I helplessly stared up at him from my position on the floor. He was so gorgeous. Sculpted perfection. I just wanted to run my hands over him everywhere and learn each ridge and divot.

My gaze landed on his hard length, which was just a bit above my head. I really wanted to learn those ridges.

Face flushed, I forced myself to look down at my paper.

"I'll be down in just a minute. I want to fix a few things on this," I said.

Naked, he grunted and walked out of the room. I gave up the pretense of working and fanned myself with the sketch pad. Holy hell. When I'd suggested what he should imagine, I hadn't expected things to escalate that quickly. I needed a cold shower. And maybe a cigarette.

After giving my flush some time to recede, I went downstairs. However, only Sophia was there with two plates set on the table. I looked at the sandwiches with as much longing as I'd recently looked at Solin.

"Bread? I'm in heaven."

Sophia grinned. "I know, right? Emily and Mary are trying to start up a bakery with the supply surplus. Right now, they're giving away what they make for free. And since Solin didn't want his, we get a little extra."

I joined her at the table, setting my sketch pad to the side.

"Where did Solin go?" I asked.

Sophia shrugged. "He didn't give me a chance to ask him. They get like that sometimes. Flighty."

I picked up my sandwich, trying not to overthink why he'd wanted to escape the house. As I adjusted my grip, I saw I was leaving behind grey fingerprints and quickly set it back down.

"I'll be right back," I said. "No eating my sandwich."

She laughed. "There's enough food that I can be picky again and say no thanks to dirty bread."

I hurried to the guest bathroom, used the toilet while I was there, then washed the graphite from my hands. It didn't take me that long, but when I returned to the kitchen and saw my sketch pad in Sophia's hands, I realized I should have skipped peeing.

Her gaze lifted to mine.

"Sorry for snooping, but I was dying to see what you two were working on. Does he know?"

"Uh, well, he posed for it, so, yeah."

She chuckled. "Not the recent ones. Does he know you've been drawing him since he helped with the wall?"

I sank into my chair. "No. When I realized he was already with someone, I kept my mouth shut. I didn't know until after I'd already agreed to sketch him. He wants a picture for you."

She flipped to the current one that was mostly finished.

"This almost makes me wish I felt something more than friendship for him. The sexual energy in this is explosive."

"Thanks. Does he know that you only think of him as a friend?"

She set the pad aside and picked up her sandwich.

"Yeah, I've told him several times. But the fey are patient, persistent, and don't mind being told 'no' a million times. If you're into him, you should make a move."

There was no denying the way my stomach fluttered with excitement at the idea of hitting on Solin. But I'd witnessed the way his gaze had heated at the mention of Sophia's name. I mean, he was getting down and dirty in front of me just so he could win her over. No matter how she felt about him, he was definitely interested in her. Could I make a move on him, knowing that it might not be welcome?

"Thanks for letting me know," I said.

"Does that mean you're going to give it a try?"

"I don't know. He really seems to like you. I've been staring at his dick for hours and don't think he's noticed my fascination. I'm not sure he'd pick up on any subtle hints that I'm into him."

"Then, don't be subtle," she said with a grin.

My nerves kicked up higher at the thought of being not subtle with Solin. I'd already fondled his dick and petted his hands. The level of don't-be-subtle he'd need might be a little too much for me to risk. It could either go very right or very, very embarrassingly wrong. Was I willing to put myself out there like that?

The door opened as I finished the last bite of my sandwich.

"Speak of the devil," Sophia said with a smirk.

When Solin walked toward us, his gaze locked with mine.

"Are you ready?"

"Hold up," Sophia said. "Before you whisk her away again for endless hours, doing your super-secret project, I want to know where you ran off to in such a hurry that you gave up your portion of bread."

"I went to speak with Shax at the practice grounds."

"You have practice grounds?" I asked. "For what?"

His gaze settled on me. I loved the way he gave his complete attention when someone spoke.

"The human females are learning to fight better there."

"I heard about it," Sophia said. "I've been working up the courage to check it out."

"Why do you need courage?" I asked.

"Eden was so sore the first time she could barely walk up the stairs the next day. Their guys really put them through the paces."

"They do not pace," Solin said.

Sophia grinned at him. "It's a figure of speech, not literal."

Solin didn't seem to care either way because he waved

for me.

"Come, Brooke. Let us continue our project."

I thanked Sophia for the sandwich and grabbed my sketch pad. Solin was already halfway up the stairs again by the time I caught up to him. This time when he undressed, I turned my back to him and looked over the art supplies. He had an emery board for fine point sharpening, a pencil extender, and a craft utility knife for rough sharpening.

"I am ready."

I swallowed hard at the sound of Solin's voice and turned around. He once again lay on his back with an arm behind his head and his far knee bent. His right hand lay on his stomach, though, as he watched me.

"Were you comfortable with the last pose?" I asked, wondering about the change.

"Yes."

He didn't say anything more or move his wayward hand. Keen disappointment shot through me. What kind of perv was I? A huge one, apparently, since I desperately wanted to watch him stroke himself again. Never mind the fact that I didn't need that part to finish the sketch.

Disappointed, but doing my best to hide it, I worked on finishing his legs. He kept moving restlessly, though.

"Can you put your leg back where it was?" I asked when he'd turned his leg enough that it was messing with the area I was working on.

"Show me."

Those words were music to my ears. I damn near threw my pencil to the floor in my rush to crawl to him. Fingers itching for a touch, I trailed them over his thigh muscle and down the side of his knee before slipping my hands under his calf and gently turning his leg in.

"Like that." I didn't back away, though. I let my hands wander some more. "Your tone is amazing. I love the way the light plays over your skin, shadowing these beautiful divots and highlighting all the ridges. So many ridges." When I realized my hands were wandering over his abs, I jerked my hand back. "Sorry. Memorizing all the contours. For the sketch."

He grunted, his unwavering gaze probably seeing every ounce of my lust for his body. If I were a dude, people would call me a pig. Oink-oink, baby. I refused to stop eye-fucking the man. It wasn't like my quiet perusal was hurting anything. Was it?

"Does it make you uncomfortable when I touch you?" I asked.

"No. I like when you show me. I want to look like sex."

"Oh, you do." I flushed at the escaped words and cleared my throat. Then busied myself with arranging his hair. There was nothing about this man that I didn't like touching. My gaze dipped to his lips.

"Do you mind if I touch your face?" I asked.

"No."

I ran my fingers over his wide brow and down his strong nose. The way his jaw muscle twitched under my fingers sent a thrill of delight through me as much as the definition of his jawline. Unable to help myself, I ran a finger along the curve of his bottom lip. It was soft and warm and begged to be kissed.

The distance between my lips and his closed, and I realized it was because I was leaning in. He watched me, his expression giving nothing away as my gaze flicked between incredible yellow-green eyes and his lips.

What would he do if I planted one on him? Sophia said not to be subtle. Could I just lean in and brush my lips against his? Should I?

CHAPTER SEVEN

LIGHTLY BRACING MY HANDS ON HIS CHEST, I THREW CAUTION TO the wind and closed the distance. The first touch of my lips to his was divine. He was soft and warm. And oh-so-welcoming. Or so I thought. It took a moment to realize he wasn't moving under me, and the muscles under my hands had tensed.

Flushing, I quickly backed off and refused to meet his gaze while I turned away under the guise of reclaiming my spot.

"Sorry. I should have asked. Yep, they're as soft as they look. I think I can draw them now."

There was a beat of silence behind me.

"Should I touch myself again?" he asked uncertainly. "For the drawing?"

I nodded dumbly when what I really needed to do was say no so I could calm the thundering race of my heart. There was no misreading the situation now. He'd tensed when I'd kissed him and had definitely not kissed back. It didn't matter if Sophia gave her blessing because she wasn't into him. Solin was too into Sophia to notice anyone else.

It was common knowledge that none of his kind were

socially adept. And they certainly weren't used to women. The poor guy was probably wondering what the hell was going on. It was kind of funny that my diminutive self could scare a guy who had the strength to rip the head off an infected. But it was the truth. Females freaked them out because they didn't want to screw up their chances to win one of their own.

Taking a slow breath, I pasted a friendly smile on my face and sat down. The moment I looked at Solin, though, in the same position from before lunch, my "be nice" attitude flew out the window. The heat in his eyes pulled me under his spell once more. I couldn't tear my gaze from the way his hand stroked his impressive length...not even if my life depended on it. Maybe it did, I admitted to myself. If I didn't find a way out of Tenacity, I'd slowly starve.

I started sketching again, my mind racing. There were always those hookup dates Emily was arranging. Maybe I could find a different fey.

"Did I move wrong?" Solin asked.

"No. You're perfect."

He stopped stroking himself and blinked at me.

"You look angry." He glanced down at his hard length then back at me. "Tell me what to do to be sexy."

Aw, hell.

"I swear you are sexy, Solin." I let my gaze skim him from head to toe. "So sexy." The sound of my own raw whisper snapped me out of my daze.

"Then why are you angry-drawing?" he asked.

Because I didn't want a new fey. I wanted the one in front of me. How could I convince him to consider me instead of Sophia?

I licked my suddenly dry lips while my brain scrambled for an answer.

"I'm having trouble getting some of the details right. I didn't want to make you uncomfortable by asking to touch you some more. You know, to better study you for the drawing. You don't have to—"

"Yes."

"Yes?"

"Yes, you may touch me. Eden told Ghua that consent needs to be clearly given. You have my consent."

"Oh. Okay. Yeah, good." Realizing I was rambling, I shut my mouth and hustled across the carpet. Where to touch? What to touch? Everything looked so damn delicious. Idly, I feathered my fingers over his abs while I mentally regrouped. I had his permission to touch him, and I needed to do it in a way that would open his eyes to me.

My gaze flicked to his massive, hard length, and my cheeks flamed as I thought of the one sure way to get a man's attention.

"Can I study the texture of your…?"

I couldn't say it, not in the middle of my self-induced heart attack.

His hand glided over his length once, then he released himself.

"Yes."

How was I still alive with my heart beating this hard? Barely breathing, I leaned closer and carefully circled my hand around his impressive girth. He watched me raptly, giving me hope that he was finally seeing me. I wanted to give him a reassuring smile but couldn't manage. My heart was beating so hard. I desperately wanted this to work.

Focusing on his thick length, I wet my lips again and closed the distance.

At the first touch of my tongue to his cock, he full-body twitched. I playfully circled the head, letting the anticipation build as my breath warmed him. When he was slick, I closed my mouth around him. He tasted like outside after the rain when it was hot and sunny again, and I couldn't get enough.

I'd barely worked my way down a third of his length before he hit my uvula. He was huge. At the thought of what he'd feel like inside of me, I groaned.

There was no answering groan. No hand on my head, encouraging me to try to go farther. Nothing.

Shit. Double shitty-shit. I backed off with a wet smack and sat back on my heels.

"Thanks. I think I can draw it now," I said, not meeting his eyes.

With the taste of him lingering on my tongue, I scuttled back to my spot and started adding intimate details to his sketch-cock. Shame burned my face as I worked. How could I be so thick? Obviously, fey were different from human guys. Just because they were obsessed with seeing a girl's privates didn't mean they were obsessed about sex. They probably just wanted to see it to appease their curiosity.

I needed a new game plan. No, I needed to know what made the gorgeous creature in front of me tick.

"What do you like about Sophia?" I asked.

"She is not angry at me."

I paused my sketch and looked up at him. He was once again stroking himself as he watched me.

"Not angry at you?"

"Humans either fear or hate fey. Sophia does neither."

Well, that didn't help me figure out how to get him to like me.

"What else do you like about her?" I asked.

He blinked at me, and I got the distinct feeling that I wouldn't be getting an answer.

"So that training ground sounded interesting. What else do you guys do around here for fun?"

"We watch the children play when they are outside, but there are few. Angel will have a baby soon and add to their numbers. She says new babies are fragile at first, and we will need to be extra careful. Many of us wish to hold the small ones. Shax is lucky to have one of his own."

"You want babies?"

"I would give my life to have a family."

My ovaries imploded.

"So you spend your free time watching the kids here and dream of having one of your own. What else?"

"What else is there?"

"Watching movies? Playing games?"

"The alcohol burns," he said with a slight frown.

I smirked, having heard how some of the girls here had invented drinking games for gambling things like supplies for kisses. Too bad those had been shut down.

"Yeah, alcohol can burn. But you can play games without drinking. Just for fun, you know?"

His hand paused on his shaft.

"If you need a break, let me know. It shouldn't take me too much longer to finish this pose."

"Take your time. What games do you play just for fun?"

"I like card games. Crazy Eights, Go Fish, War."

"I want to learn War."

I grinned at his determined response.

"It's a fairly easy game. I'm sure Sophia can show you."

"I want you to show me."

My heart gave an erratic beat, and I felt my cheeks heating, which was kind of ridiculous considering where my mouth had been a minute ago. My stomach gave a flip at the memory and what his sudden chattiness and change in preference might mean. Maybe my extreme pass had worked.

Or maybe he thought he could have a little booty on the side while he still played for Sophia.

I punched my inner pessimist in the chesticles and kept sketching.

"If you have a deck of cards and Sophia's up for company after dinner, I'll teach you."

He grunted, and a thoughtful look shadowed his face as he idly stroked a cock that showed no signs of flagging.

"You like the food here." Even though he said it like a statement, it seemed more like a question to me.

"What's not to like?" I said with a small laugh. "I haven't had eggs or bread in months."

"What do you eat?"

"Corn," I said with a teasing grin.

His lips actually twitched in return.

"Truthfully, I eat whatever I'm given. Some days, it's a sleeve of stale crackers. And I'm grateful for each one. Other days, people pool their ingredients together and make stews or soups to share. It's a lot of canned vegetables. I think that's part of the reason I'm excited to welcome spring. I'd like to eat something green that's not mushy, you know?" I laughed lightly and shook my head. "Well, maybe you don't. You prefer mostly meat, right?"

"Yes," he said.

Something indistinguishable crossed his expression. Did he think I was judging him?

"I like meat too. It's a little hard to come by now, though."

His expression shuttered more and not in a good way. Worried I was losing the footing I'd gained with him, I glanced down at the sketch and tried to regroup. His expression on the paper was still off. The memory of how he'd looked was forever burned into my brain. Hot. Sexy as hell. Lickable to the point I'd wanted to jump him. But also carefree in a way he wasn't now.

I knew exactly what he needed.

"You're doing great," I said. "We're almost done. I just need a little more from you if you're willing."

"I am."

"Good. Keep your head turned toward me and think of Sophia again."

The smooth rhythm of his hand faltered, and I rushed to paint the picture for him.

"Imagine her mouth against yours. The wet heat of a tongue running over your bottom lip and hands running over your skin. Down your stomach."

His expression and breathing changed. That desperate need was back.

"That's perfect, Solin. Absolutely perfect."

I was panting right along with him as I hurried to capture his expression. When I finished, I didn't stop to admire my work. I turned the page and started another one. It felt like my hand was moving a mile a minute to recreate the pose. Only, this picture didn't have a trail of pre-cum glistening along the back of his hand, and his eyes weren't open and focused on me. Making small changes, I worked to recreate the moment he came.

As I sketched, I encouraged him to keep going, only partially aware of what I was saying.

"I know your arm's probably getting tired, but this is beautiful, Solin. And so incredibly hot…"

"Anyone who sees this is going to want to climb in your bed…"

"I could just lick you right now…"

He grunted, and the tips of his ears darkened. A moment later, he came with far more force than the first time. I watched in rapture, my core clenching with each pulsing release.

When he finished, we exhaled in unison.

"That was incredible."

I quickly looked down at the sketch to hide my flush and scrambled to find something a little less desperate to say.

"I have two really good options for you. Go ahead and clean up. I'll show them to you when you're done."

He used his shirt again, wiping his chest, and he got to his feet. I lost the battle to not look up and swallowed hard at the sight of his still semi-hard length.

"Thank you, Brooke," he said before walking out of the room.

I stared after him and made a pained face. I wanted Solin so bad it hurt.

CHAPTER EIGHT

Unable to sit still, I went downstairs and found Sophia sprawled out on the couch, watching a movie. She paused it when she heard me and gave me a questioning look. I shook my head but didn't let her pitying expression get me down.

"Would you happen to have a deck of cards? Solin wants to learn how to play War."

"Sure." She sprang up from her spot. "I found some in the drawer." She produced two well-worn decks and grinned at me. "You teach him, and I'll cook dinner. I play the winner."

It didn't take long for Solin to rejoin us. A clean, white shirt stretched across the expanse of his chest, perfectly outlining his impressive pectorals. His shoulders were made for grabbing on and clinging to for dear life. I openly stared as I let myself imagine the activities that would require clinging until a thump brought me out of my stupor.

Flushing, I hurried to pick up the cards from the floor and held them out to him.

"Ready to learn?"

He nodded.

While Sophia moved around in the kitchen, Solin and I sat at the table, and I started explaining the game. He was quick to pick up the concept, but it took a little while for him to memorize the "symbols" on the cards. Once he did, though, it was fun.

I went a step further by teaching him Slapjack. Oh, he loved that one.

The sound of his hand coming down on the table was like a crack of thunder. His triumphant grins were even better. However, with his faster reflexes, it wasn't as fun when he kept beating me. We adjusted the rules to include a one second delay on his part, which gave me a fighting chance.

Sophia joined the fun when dinner was done. I ate my portion while she and Solin faced off. I couldn't decide what was better. The way he kept mercilessly beating her or the casserole she'd made for us.

We played several rounds before I reluctantly said it was time for me to leave. Sophia gave me a sad wave goodbye as I headed out the door with Solin. While he and I walked to the wall, I considered what else I could do to show him that I was into him.

I'd heard that the fey were hard to shake once they had their sights set on a girl, but I'd also heard that it wasn't impossible to win one of them away from his target. Angel had managed it. But she was pregnant—the second holy grail for the fey, a baby, as Solin had confirmed. Since I wasn't growing one of those, I was out of luck for that as a lure.

We reached the wall, and he respectfully asked if he could carry me, just like he'd done every night. Out of the shadows, several other fey emerged. Our escorts. Or, rather, my escorts.

Safely in Solin's arms, I didn't fear the dark as he left the protection of the wall. Well, I did a little. I knew what was out there and was smart enough to fear the infected and the hellhounds. But I knew that Solin and the others would keep me safe.

I turned my face into his chest and breathed in deeply. He smelled so amazing. What did I have to do to get his attention? I leaned my forehead against him and felt his arms tighten around me slightly. Was that a good thing or a bad thing though? Like was he pre-throw-the-Brooke tensing or me-likey tensing? It was so hard to tell with these fey.

My stomach plunged to my toes as he jumped, a signal that we'd reached Tenacity.

"Tell me where you live," Solin said instead of letting me down.

I smiled up at him.

"It's okay. I don't mind walking."

He grunted and set me on my feet.

"I will walk with you."

That suited me just fine because I didn't really want an audience when I showed him his two sketch options. As we walked the streets, we earned a few dirty looks from the people we passed. There weren't many out, but it still reminded me of Solin's comment about so many people hating on him. It made my heart hurt for him.

"This is where I'm staying," I said, stopping in front of the two-story house. "That room right there." I pointed to the lit window. "Sam's probably up reading. It's her thing. I think it helps her escape reality for a bit. Same as drawing does for me."

I checked to make sure no one was close by then opened the sketchpad to show him the first picture.

"This is option A." I flipped to the next one. "And this is the other option. You look amazing in both of them."

I looked up at him and found him watching me. Doubt crept in, and I looked at both sketches.

"Were you hoping for something else?"

"No. They are perfect. I will take the first one."

My heart gave a leap of joy because I really loved the second one.

Carefully tearing the sketch free, I handed it over to him.

"Thanks for trusting me to do the sketch. Maybe I'll see you around?"

He tilted his head at me like I'd just said the most puzzling thing.

"I will be here in the morning. You will teach me to sketch."

I grinned so wide I was pretty sure I was flashing some molars.

"I can't wait. See you tomorrow."

That whole rule about not looking back and showing you're interested or desperate was dumb. I was both and wanted him to know it. So I looked over my shoulder about every two feet and again when I reached the door. He didn't move from where I'd left him, his gaze remaining locked on me.

I gave a little wave and slipped inside.

"We didn't save you anything," Wayne said from the kitchen.

Terri's expression conveyed her apology. I didn't acknowledge it. Her husband Wayne was a big enough dick that he'd call her out for her sympathy.

"Don't worry about it. I ate in Tolerance."

"I'm sure you did. What'd you have to do to earn it?"

I rolled my eyes at him and kicked off my shoes.

"Nothing gross if that's what you're trying to insinuate." I would have liked to tell him to pull the stick out of his ass. But I didn't. It was people like him who drove the wedge between the humans and fey, resulting in our current state of not enough supplies. Making waves just made more trouble, and I wanted less.

"You can eat my share tomorrow too. I'll be teaching sketching and eating three meals in pay. Fair trade and nothing that requires giving my vagina a workout. Have a good night."

I grinned as I walked away. Little waves were satisfying.

Sam was in bed as I predicted. She looked up from her book as I closed the door behind me.

"What'd they feed you today?"

"Scrambled eggs with corned beef hash. At least a cup of each. It was so good." I sat on my bed. "And real sandwiches for lunch. Ham and cheese. I don't know where they got it from, but it melted in my mouth. And the bread was fresh and soft and smelled yeasty."

She made a sad face, which I knew was bread-envy.

"And a casserole for dinner. It had onions and meat and noodles and peas."

"Sometimes, I hate you for being so brave," she said.

"There's no bravery required. The fey are really nice, Sam."

"Tell that to the people they killed."

"They didn't know what they were doing. And look at how our military tried to kill the fey. Isn't that the problem here? Everyone thinking different is bad and scary and needs to die."

"Next, you're going to be saying you want a hellhound for a pet."

"Don't be crazy. But also don't let fear hold you back. The fey are kind, Sam, and you'd be well-fed if you just gave one of them a chance."

She picked up her book, and I knew she was hiding again. That was fine. I didn't want to stay up and talk too long anyway. Tomorrow would be another chance for me to persuade Solin, and I wanted to be well-rested for it.

Crawling under the covers fully clothed and with my jacket still on, I closed my eyes and thought back to how I'd learned to sketch. A lot of it had been intuitive, but I'd watched a few videos on techniques along the way.

A sound from above had me opening my eyes at the same time Sam whispered, "Did you hear that?"

"I did." I rolled toward her and saw the fear in her eyes. We'd been in Whiteman for more security breaches than either of us wanted to remember. "It's not what you think," I said calmly. "We're not right next to the wall. And if a guard spotted something, they'd yell."

"You're not supposed to be here. Go home!"

Sam's eyes rounded at the faint echo from outside.

"It's one of *them*," she whispered, her fear fading. "On *our* roof."

Pulling my covers up high, I hid my growing smile.

CHAPTER NINE

I WASN'T WELL-RESTED. MY EYES FELT HOT AND GRITTY WHEN I opened them to dawn's first light. A groan escaped me.

"Too early," Sam mumbled, burrowing deeper under her covers.

Solin—at least, I think it had been Solin—hadn't left after he'd first been spotted. Instead, based on the yelling, he'd disappeared for a time only to reappear just when I was on the verge of going back to sleep. The on and off interruptions throughout the night hadn't only kept me up but Sam as well.

"If you sleep in, you'll miss your portion of breakfast," I reminded her as I wearily pulled myself from bed.

She moaned but started moving, too.

After waiting my turn for the bathroom and foregoing a tepid shower, I grabbed a clean change of clothes. Not only was I going to eat Solin and Sophia's food today, but I also planned to hog their hot water.

Outside, I saw I wasn't the only early riser up and about. Clusters of people spoke in groups on our street. Based on the angry gestures toward the roofs, I guessed they were bitching about last night's fey visitor. I wanted to roll my eyes. They got their panties in a twist over the dumbest things. A fey was on a few roofs. Who cared? A fey presence usually meant more protection or more food. What was there to bitch about?

"Anyone find a gift basket on their front step?" I called loudly. "I'm willing to take any nasty fey food off your hands."

Two ladies snorted and hid their laughs. One guy flipped me off. Another agreed with me and said that any food donated by the fey should be shared.

Smirking that I'd distracted them from their pointless hate, I continued toward the wall. Solin already waited just inside. No other fey were with him, which was probably the reason Matt was speaking to him in low tones.

As soon as he saw me, Solin gave up any pretense of listening to Matt. Gaze locked with mine, he watched my approach, and my pulse sped up at the predatory glint in his eyes.

I really hoped I wasn't seeing things.

"Good morning, Matt. Solin, you're here early."

Rather than admitting he'd been on the roofs last night, he planted a seed of doubt by not acknowledging my comment at all.

"Are you ready to leave?" I glanced at Matt. "Do you need another minute?"

Matt sighed and shook his head.

"No, I'll talk to Ryan when he gets here."

The way he said it gave me an uh-oh feeling.

"Is someone in trouble?"

"Not yet. I'm just worried that more unannounced late-night visits might end with someone accidentally shot. More likely, it'll be the people trying to sleep peacefully in their homes catching a stray bullet meant for someone else."

I looked at Solin, who still watched me intently, and had the feeling he wasn't really understanding Matt's message. Hopefully, Ryan would. I really didn't want to get shot in my sleep because of some asshole's stray bullet meant for a fey.

"Okay. Then, I guess I'm ready."

Solin had me up in his arms before I could blink. With my bundle of things clutched to my chest, I turned my face into his chest as he took off running. The heat he radiated warmed my nose as I unabashedly breathed him in. I couldn't wait to get back to—

I frowned as I realized there would be no naked sketching today. No watching him stroke himself. I leaned further into his chest and brushed my face against his pec. *I'll miss you, my beauty.*

Too soon, my stomach did a flip to signal Solin had cleared Tolerance's wall, and I lifted my head.

"I'll walk from here," I said before he could keep jogging.

After a grunt, he put me down.

"So, what should we do first? Want to start with perspective, which would be things like drawing this street and noting how the angles of the lines change the closer they are versus when they're farther away? Or should we start with shading and how that gives a drawing depth? The wall would be a good place for that."

"Did you eat already?" he asked.

"No."

"Then, first, we eat." His hard stare made me grin.

"If you're waiting for me to argue, you're going to be waiting a long time. I'm too smart to say no to food. Feed me, and I'm your friend for life."

He blinked at me, grunted, then started walking. I jogged to keep up.

"What do you want to do after we eat?"

"Learn to sketch like you do, feed you more, play Slapjack, and..." He glanced at me.

Something about that look had my toes curling and my pulse beating hard again.

"And what?" I pressed.

"More sketching."

"Sounds good to me. You'll need a lot of practice. It might come naturally to some degree, but like any skill, it takes work to refine. So don't be hard on yourself if your first few sketches look like stick figures with weird appendages. We all start somewhere."

His steps slowed, and he glanced at me.

"I will try not to be hard for the first few sketches."

Even though I knew he wasn't talking about his dick, the way he'd worded it had my mind going there.

"You'll be fine," I said, patting his arm.

He opened the door for me, and I grinned as I stepped inside.

"Sweetheart, I'm home!"

Sophia's laugh echoed in the space.

"About damn time. It was awfully lonely without you two. I hope you're both hungry."

"Starving," I called back, hurrying to ditch my jacket on the coat rack before joining her in the kitchen. Breathing in deeply, I tried to guess what she'd made as she removed three plates from the oven.

"Bacon? It smells like bacon. And onions."

She smirked at me.

"Any reason you're so hungry?"

"Uh, because the assholes in my house have a rule about being present for the assigned meal times. If you're not there, you forfeit the food. And to be extra dickish, they don't make breakfast until after the morning shift change. It's just an extra excuse not to go out on the supply runs."

She made a face then glanced at Solin, who'd sat beside me at the table.

"I'm so glad I wound up here. Plenty of food and warmth. Usually enough company. It was a little weird that you didn't come home last night, Solin. I thought maybe you stayed with Brooke, which would be totally fine with me since we both know that you and I are only friends, right?"

Solin's gaze darted between us, the panicked look in his eyes saying as much as the darkening tips of his ears. I just wished I could read his mind so I knew how exactly to translate all those cues. Was he nervous and blushing because he still wanted to give her the picture and she'd just thoroughly friend-zoned him in front of me? Or did he not want to admit to last night's light stalkery? Or worse yet, was it a combination of both? Maybe he'd only been on the roof because he was worried about me and didn't want to admit it to Sophia if he still held out hope for her. Ugh. This sucked.

"Whatever you made for breakfast smells amazing. End the suspense, and show off your creation," I said to distract us all from the increasingly uncomfortable conversation. I would be better equipped to deal with it once I was fed.

"Bacon, onion, and cheese omelets with toast and hash browns."

"I hope this meal comes with a bib because I'm drooling," I said, enthusiastically grabbing my fork as she set down my warm plate.

I groaned around my first mouthful. Sophia laughed and joined me. Neither of us tried to make conversation as I worked my way around my plate. After I swallowed my last bite, I leaned back with a sigh.

"Every night, my roommate waits up for me to hear what I ate. She's either going to stop talking to me or give in and go on one of those fey dates that Emily is setting up."

"I hope she goes for the dating option. It'd be sad if food jealousy wrecks a friendship."

I snorted.

"Food envy is doing a lot more than wrecking friendships in Tenacity. That place is a powder keg. Matt's doing his best to keep it in check, but eventually, it's going to blow. And when it does, it won't be pretty."

"Hopefully, you won't still be there when that happens," Sophia said meaningfully.

I nodded but said nothing. Whether or not I remained in Tenacity was up to me and the effort I put into winning Solin over. I glanced at his empty plate and noted his ears were no longer dark at the tips.

"Ready?" I asked.

He grunted and stood.

"Brooke and I will be in my room."

"Your room?" I asked. "There will be more for you to draw outside."

"It's too cold outside for you." He turned and started walking away.

With a quick shrug at Sophia, I followed in his wake. He was at the art table, looking at the pencils, when I entered his room. I helped him pick out a pad, briefly explaining the differences in the papers he'd found, and a pencil. He listened with complete focus as I went through some of the basics to sketches and impressed me with his realistic sketch of the pencil I'd set on the windowsill.

With the decent view from his room, I told him to draw what he saw before excusing myself to search out Sophia. She already had the dishes washed and put away when I found her on the couch, reading a book.

"You remind me of Sam," I said, looking down at her. "She's always reading too."

"I don't blame her. Books are a perfect escape from reality. They're also keeping me from becoming unattractively bald because I'm close to pulling out my hair in boredom."

"The fey would still hit on you if you were bald."

"They would," she agreed with a grin. "Why are you down here and not up there with Solin? Not that I mind the company."

"I wanted to ask if I could use your shower and washer. I also wanted to ask about last night. Did he ever come back after leaving with me?"

She grinned and shook her head as she got up to show me where the washer and dryer were.

"He left with you and came back with you. But I'm guessing he didn't stay with you?"

"Nope. Sam and I heard something on the roof, and there was a ton of yelling after that. Kept us up half the night."

"Explains the dark circles and bloodshot eyes. The shower will help with that. Walking back into that room wrapped in nothing but a towel will help with the rest."

"Tempting, but you saw his reaction at the table. I still can't figure out if he's into me or not. He's hard to read."

"He didn't come home last night, Brooke. He's into you. Trust me. Skip the clothes and wear the towel."

"I'll think about it."

After stripping down to nothing and tossing it all in the washer, I took my time in the bathroom. It'd been ages since I'd taken a relaxing shower with no one telling me to hurry up or fearing for my life. I exhaled and soaked up the moment. If I played my cards right, maybe I'd have a lot more long, hot showers in my future.

Once I was finished, I brushed my wet hair and wrapped myself in the fluffy grey towel Sophia had left for me. I stared at myself in the mirror for a moment. The towel covered everything, showing my creamy shoulders and pronounced clavicles and a few inches above the knees to my toes. It wasn't much skin. Would it be enough?

There was only one way to find out.

Foregoing a pep talk, I left the bathroom and made my way upstairs, ignoring Sophia's knowing smirk. Solin was where I'd left him. Sitting in front of the window, sketching away. He looked up when he heard me. His ears immediately started to darken.

I gave him a reassuring smile and looked at his sketch. There were a few places where he'd gone a little too dark and some missing details in others, but overall, it was impressive.

"That's amazing," I said. "I think you're a natural."

"Does that mean I can sketch you now?"

CHAPTER TEN

"ME?" I ASKED, NOT BELIEVING MY EARS.

He stood and went to the mattress.

"Lie down like this."

My pulse jumped with excitement until I saw the pose he wanted. Just me on the mattress, arms at my sides and legs disappointingly closed.

"Um. Okay."

I briefly considered flashing him my fun zone as I got down onto the mattress, but he wasn't even watching me. He was playing with his damn pencil. The one filled with graphite, not the one filled with infection-inoculating baby batter.

"Close your eyes," he said, once I was in place.

Withholding a sigh, I quickly complied and waited to see what he'd do next. The scratch of the pencil against the paper filled the room. Time stretched. He didn't say anything. He didn't turn the page. Just scratch, scratch, scratch. I couldn't really be disappointed. It was a sound I loved because I knew the joy of creating an image. Sure, I'd hoped for more. But if I was helping him discover a love of art, that was just as good. At least, that was what I told myself as I yawned and relaxed into the mattress.

I didn't know I'd drifted off until I heard Sophia laughing and something touched my nose.

Blinking open my eyes, I focused on her blurry face.

"What are you doing?"

"I'm interfering. Your man left."

"What?"

I sat up quickly, noticing the light blanket covering me and the way my towel fell open underneath.

"Damn. Missed opportunity," I muttered, tucking it around me.

"Maybe, maybe not," Sophia said, sitting on the mattress beside me. "Check these out."

She handed me a sketchbook. I flipped it open, seeing his first sketches out the window. Then me lying on the mattress. He'd spent a good deal of time on it, shading and detailing my features so realistically that all I could do was stare. Like I'd done for his session, he'd added sketches of my lips, my ear, and my profile.

"Wow," I breathed. "He's really good."

"Keep going. He gets better."

"Really?"

I turned the page and burst out laughing.

It was an up close and personal view of my ungroomed mound peeking out from under the towel and mostly hidden by my firmly closed thighs.

"That's a lot of hair. Well past time for some clamscaping."

"Shut up," I said with a laugh. "At least he looked. That's something, right? Why did he take off though?"

She shrugged.

"He was out the door before I even realized he was

downstairs. I was in the kitchen, finishing up lunch. You hungry?"

"Always."

"Your clothes are done if you want to get dressed."

We enjoyed lunch together, speculating why Solin had left and analyzing his reactions to my passes so far.

"Seriously? You went down on him, and he did nothing?"

"Nothing. No hand on the back of my head. No groan. Not a twitch."

"But he didn't pull away or tell you to stop or go soft. So that's something. You should have just told him you thought he was the sexiest man you'd ever seen and you want to have his feybies."

I rolled my eyes at her.

"You've seen how strong these guys are. The last thing I wanted to do was scare him to the point that he'd toss me out the window."

"He wouldn't do that."

"Wouldn't he if he thought I was trying to steal him away from the woman of his dreams?"

She huffed a sigh and used her last french fry to mop up the remaining ketchup on her plate.

"Maybe we should just have a group sit down when he gets back. I can tell him I'm not interested but you are, and I fully support you giving him blow jobs. No window tossing."

I laughed and shook my head.

"Let's hold off on an intervention until we know why he left."

We didn't have to wait long. Solin returned with a box of supplies before I dried the last plate.

"What's all that?" Sophia asked as he set the box on the counter.

I didn't look at what he had but how he watched me. His gaze swept over my face, and his ears darkened slightly.

"It is what you need to make mac and cheese with chopped pickles topped with a buttery tortilla chip crumble for dinner."

A smile lit my face as I looked at Sophia.

"It's my favorite food."

"Girl, I'm only making that if you promise to introduce him to some queefcake for dessert."

"Is queefcake your favorite dessert?" Solin asked.

"No, but I bet it'll be yours," Sophia said before she broke down and laughed so hard she wheezed.

"Ignore her. Thank you for finding everything to make my favorite food. That's really sweet of you."

His ears darkened further.

"Come. I want to draw some more." He turned and walked away from me, missing my growing smile.

"Go get 'em tiger," Sophia whispered with a grin.

I shook my head at her and hurried to follow in his wake. He moved fast though and was already seated in his spot by the window when I entered.

"I'm sorry I fell asleep before."

"You were tired and needed the rest." He frowned slightly. "Are you still tired? Or hungry?"

"No. But aren't you hungry? You skipped lunch."

"I want to draw more. Do you remember the pose?"

Humoring him, I lay down on the mattress and assumed the same position.

"I can do a different pose if you want."

"No."

There was a faint scratch, scratch, scratch on the paper for a moment.

"I can't see your legs or arms. The clothes are in the way."

Grinning, I stood up and quickly took off my pants and my shirt. When my hands went to my underwear, he stopped me.

"That's enough. Lie down."

Pouting on the inside, I returned to my place.

I'd touched him. I'd kissed him. I'd even sucked his impressively delicious length. If that didn't say, "hey, I like everything about you," I didn't know what did.

Direct didn't work. Maybe subtle would.

"I saw your pictures," I said after the silence stretched into several minutes.

He grunted.

"They were *both* really good. I've never had an erotic picture done of me before. Would you like to try to do a full one?"

The scratching stopped, and I lifted my head to look at him. Dark grey colored his ears from tip to base, spreading into his cheeks. He was, without a doubt, the most adorable fey in all of Tolerance.

"Yes," he said after a moment.

This time, when I reached for my underwear, he didn't stop me.

Not only did I take it off, I tossed it at him so it landed on his paper. I did the same with my sport bra. For a moment, he didn't move. Then he inhaled deeply. The way he held my gaze while doing so brought on a full-body flush that grew hotter when he picked up both pieces of material and set them aside.

Heart racing, I sat back on my heels.

"How do you want me?" I asked.

"To look like sex, you need to touch yourself."

Did those words sound strained? With the blood rushing in my ears, I wasn't sure.

"Like this?" I trailed my fingers between my breasts and down to my navel.

He slowly shook his head. I pursed my lips thoughtfully for a moment before spreading my knees and running my fingers over my thighs.

"Like this?"

Without looking away from me, he grabbed my sketchpad and flipped it open.

"Like this."

He turned the pad to show me the picture of him jacking off. It took everything in me not to laugh and cheer like a crazy woman. I took two calming breaths before answering.

"I can do that."

Hands trembling, I eased back onto the mattress, pillowed my head with my left arm while bending the knee of my left leg. His gaze remained locked on me as I allowed that knee to fall to the side slightly and reached between my legs.

He leaned forward as I touched the hair he'd drawn in such detail.

He stopped breathing when I parted myself.

The first circle of my finger around my clit?

The pencil in his hand snapped in two.

"Would it make you uncomfortable if I touched you?" he asked. "To better study you for the drawing."

It was my turn to swallow hard.

"You can touch me however you like," I said.

He rose in one smooth motion only to crouch beside me. His gaze swept over my face, lingering on each feature. He took his time studying me. If not for his question, I would have doubted he meant to touch me and gotten impatient.

Instead, I waited.

He didn't disappoint. However, he did surprise me. Instead of touching my face, he reached for my hand, which I'd forgotten between my legs.

Lifting it, he ran his fingers over the pads of mine. Then he brought them to his lips. The temperature in the room spiked ten degrees when he opened his mouth and gently sucked the tip of my middle finger. The one that had been circling my clit.

I couldn't look away from him.

He didn't look away from me.

His tongue teased the pad of my finger before he released it and set my hand on my chest. His fingers drifted between my breasts and stroked my soft stomach. Rather than going any lower, he stayed there, drifting back and forth a few times just below my navel.

He finally looked away from my face, gaze drifting to his hand.

"I wanted to remember," he said. "That's why I drew you."

His hand moved upward until he touched the edge of my hand that rested just below my breast.

"I should have asked first."

"It's okay. I'm not mad," I breathed.

CHAPTER ELEVEN

HE LIFTED HIS HAND FROM MY STOMACH AND GENTLY TRACED MY eyebrows and down the line of my nose. I smiled slightly, enjoying the way he was exploring me.

"Does touching make you uncomfortable?" he asked.

"No. I like it. It's been a long time since someone touched me like this."

"You were the first one to touch me," he said. "I liked it."

That simple admission caused a whole lot of guilt and enough uncertainty that I caught his hand in mine and sat up.

"Solin, I like you. I liked you the first time I saw you. You were lifting a car into place. Another fey said something to you, which made you smirk. You caught my attention by just being you. I really like you touching me, and I would love if this turned into something more. But I don't want to be your booby prize."

His gaze immediately shifted to my breasts.

"You do not want me to touch them?"

"No. I mean, yes, I do, but no, that's not what I meant."

He blinked at me, and I knew I was losing him.

"I don't want you to like me because I was the first girl to touch you. I want you to like me for me. It would break my heart if you keep touching me like you are and later on decide you want someone else. Do you understand what I'm saying?"

He nodded and gently nudged me back onto the mattress.

"When Angel offered to help Shax win Hannah's heart, he thought only of his need for Hannah." Solin's fingers skimmed my collarbones. "He told me he was foolish and blind until Angel opened his heart and showed him the truth." Solin shifted his attention lower, and the barely-there caress along the side of my breast made my pulse stutter. "Nice isn't enough."

Hope expanded in my chest as he held my gaze and leaned in closer.

"I want more than nice, Brooke."

I licked my lips and nodded, trying to breathe through the flush he'd ignited with his admission. His gaze shifted to my lips, and his thumb brushed against the corner of my mouth.

"I didn't see you, but now I do."

He closed the distance and brushed his lips against mine, a whisper of contact that kindled our need for each other. With a groan, he smoothed his hand along my hair and nipped my bottom lip. I licked him in return, our tongues touching. A rumbling growl echoed in the room and sent a shock straight to my core. His grip on my hair tightened, and he invaded, hungry and demanding, yet gentle.

I curled my fingers in his hair and gave as good as I got.

For several moments, the world and all of its new horrors and obstacles fell away. It was just the two of us. In a room. Alone. And one of us was wearing far too many clothes.

Turning my head, I broke away from the kiss to tell him that.

However, he robbed me of the ability to speak by taking a nipple into his mouth. I arched into the sensation, panting. He didn't give me long to catch my breath before he hungrily returned to my mouth.

His hand caught mine, and he placed my fingers between my legs.

"Show me," he whispered before backing away.

I swallowed hard and struggled to not shake as I understood what he wanted from me. Heart hammering and skin flushed, I held his gaze and touched myself again. My lips parted, and my breathing quickened as I circled my clit. He glanced down briefly and something flickered in his gaze. I wasn't sure if I was projecting my need for him or if that was really what I saw because he stood and returned to his spot.

He picked up his sketchpad and pencil, his focus alternating between me and the paper as he sketched. The rush of pleasure I'd felt with him next to me slowly faded, and doubt crept in. Oh, I knew he was interested in me now, but I felt a little silly. I mean, watching him masturbate had been hot. This didn't feel hot.

I faltered and cringed. He noticed.

"Sorry," I whispered, trying again.

Setting the pad aside, he returned to my side and picked up my stilled hand. He ran his fingers over the back.

"I've never felt anything so soft," he said. "I could touch you for days and never want to stop."

The heat flooded back in, and I smiled at him.

"I'd like it if you touched me for days."

He lifted my hand to his lips and sucked my middle finger into his mouth. My breath caught at the first touch of his tongue stroking over the surface. The brush of his fingers over my nipple had me closing my eyes and arching my hips.

Releasing my hand, his mouth took over where his fingers had played. He scraped his teeth over my tender peak, and I panted.

"The other one too," I begged.

He didn't immediately listen, still deliciously tormenting the first one. As he suckled, he tugged my hand down between my legs. I didn't need more encouragement than that. Circling my swollen nub, I pressed my free hand to the back of his head to hold him to me.

After giving equal attention to the other breast, he pulled back and looked down at me.

"You are beautiful, Brooke. Don't stop showing me," he said. "Use your pretty fingers so I can taste them again."

I closed my eyes and continued to do as he'd asked as he moved away from me. My skin tingled where he'd touched me, and I could feel how wet I was. Not letting the scratch of pencil to paper distract me, I focused on how he'd watched me. The hungry look in his eyes.

My breathing became erratic. I forgot about the pose and let my knees fall apart. Pressing and circling, I brought myself closer to the edge. It wasn't enough though.

I hovered there at the brink, hips arching, legs twitching, until frustration had me removing my hand and opening my eyes.

"Brooke?"

I realized what I'd done and blushed profusely.

"Sorry. I just need a second," I said, starting to get back into the pose.

Hands captured my knees, preventing me from closing my legs. I lifted my head and saw him leaning on the end of the mattress. This time, his gaze wasn't on my eyes and there was no mistaking the hunger in his expression.

He dipped his head and ran his tongue along the crease of my thigh and hip. A strangled noise escaped me.

"More," I breathed.

He moved to the other side and licked there too. I whimpered, and my hips bucked. If he didn't put his mouth where I needed it, I was going to die.

Reaching down, I tried to grab for his head. Instead, my fingers brushed along the edge of his pointed ear.

He growled, low and deep.

That was the only warning I had before his lips clamped over my clit, and he began to suckle like he had with my nipple. His hot mouth was relentless, and the flick of his tongue pushed me headlong over the edge.

"Ahh-rahh!"

As my insides began to spasm, he thrust a finger inside of me and curled it, hitting a sweet spot I didn't know I had. Another strangled noise escaped me. He continued to suckle and press in all the right ways to draw out the best orgasm of my life.

Trembling and weak, I lay on the mattress in a puddle of what's-my-name as I tried to catch my breath. The post-sex haze held as my pulse gradually slowed and my skin began to cool. It was only then that I registered the scratch of pencil against paper.

"Sorry I messed up the first pose," I said, sounding drunk.

"Shh. Hold still."

I smiled dreamily, more than happy to stay right where I was and remember the amazing use of his tongue.

"I'm not sure I could move if I tried. That was wonderful. Thank you."

The scratching paused.

"Can I touch you again?"

"You don't have to ask. You can touch me any time you want. Although, I might need another minute before you—"

A yip escaped me as he pressed a kiss to my clit and moved lower to lave my opening.

"Or we can just go right back at it," I breathed, already cradling his head in my hands and rolling my hips. "You have good ideas."

He grunted against me, which made me smile and play with his ear. His licking grew more aggressive. I whimpered as the need rekindled. When my hips started moving too much, his big hands pressed down on my thighs and held me in place. I couldn't stop the squeaks and squeals pouring from me.

"I love this. I really do. But I want you inside of me this time," I panted when I was close.

He lifted his head and looked down at me. Holding my gaze, he slowly penetrated me with one thick, long finger. I groaned and opened my mouth to tell him that wasn't what I meant, but the addition of a second finger stole that thought.

"Yes," I breathed, grinding down on him.

He lightly flicked his tongue over my clit, the thrusts picking up speed.

"Yes," I said again, moving with him.

Pleasure built again, and at the last minute, I remembered what I'd wanted to say. How I'd wanted this to end. I opened my mouth to tell him to wait just as he twisted his fingers inside of me and clamped his lips over my swollen nub.

A cry ripped out of me, and I arched like I was being electrocuted, convulsing with pleasure instead of pain. The keening sound of my joy echoed throughout the room until it slowly faded to a sigh. He withdrew his fingers and trailed kisses inside my thighs. I couldn't move. Or talk. Or form any thoughts outside of how completely amazing I felt because of him.

So I lay with my eyes closed again, lingering in a bliss filled haze as he gently touched my legs and hands and hair.

The scratch of pencil to paper didn't even register.

CHAPTER TWELVE

GRADUALLY, MY FACULTIES RETURNED ENOUGH THAT I HEARD HIM drawing. I knew I probably had a dopey expression and a full-body flush. Didn't care. He was a miracle maker. Twice. One right after the other. I wasn't that kind of girl. Well, I didn't used to be. I was now, though. Or at least I wanted to be.

Lifting my head, I looked at him.

"How do you feel about cuddling?" I asked.

He stopped sketching to blink at me.

"It's usually something girls like to do after what we just did."

He tossed the sketchpad aside and joined me on the mattress. Instead of pulling me into his arms, he lay on his side and trailed his fingers down my neck and over my collarbones.

"Will you stay?" he asked.

"Stay? You mean the night?"

"No. Forever."

A stupid grin tugged at my lips.

"Is this your way of asking me to be your girlfriend?"

He grunted but looked away from me. My humor faded.

"Solin, we haven't been great at communicating with each other. I should have been upfront with you when you found me on the sidewalk. I came here to look for you." I sat up and grabbed my sketchpad, flipping to the earliest pictures of him. "I started sketching you the first day I saw you in Tenacity and haven't stopped since. Not even once you were gone. I wanted to find you because I wanted to get to know you. I was hoping for a relationship.

"I get that all of this is really new to you and the rest of the fey, so I'm not pushing for anything. Just hoping, you know? But if I say or do something that bothers you, you need to be straight with me. I might get mad or hurt, but communicating clearly now will save us both a lot of heartache and frustration later. Does that make sense?"

"Yes."

"Good. Then, were you asking me to be your girlfriend just now?"

"No."

"Ouch. Okay. That does sting a little, but I appreciate your honesty." I reached for my shirt, but he tugged it from my grasp.

"I understand what girlfriend means. You can leave when you are angry or grow tired of me. I want permanent. I want the ring."

I stared at him, thoughts colliding in my head. First, he was fucking adorable. Second, he might have just proposed to me. Third, and most likely, he'd just hinted that he wanted me to propose to him.

A slow grin parted my lips, and I let go of the shirt.

"So when you said you want me to stay forever, you really meant it."

"Yes."

I stood and went to the art supplies, bending over to remove the twisty tie from around the paint brushes. A very large hand stroked my hip and gave it an experimental squeeze. I grinned, staying bent at the waist while I quickly created a loop. Another hand joined the first, holding me in place as his thumbs stroked over my skin.

"We're going to get back to this position. I promise," I said, straightening and turning at the same time. "But I have something to ask you first."

Still grinning, I got down on one knee and held up the twisty-ring.

"Solin, will you be my man forever? You can call yourself my husband, which entitles you to taking out the trash, shoveling snow from the sidewalks, and killing any bug I say needs killing. It also means, if you take this ring and put it on, that you're saying our relationship is permanent. No leaving when you're angry and tough luck if you get tired of me. We'll still need to try to do what we can to make the other person happy."

He took the ring, slid it on his third finger, and helped me to my feet.

"I'm yours."

"Yeah, you are. And what would you like to do as a newly established couple? Hint, it should involve you wearing way fewer clothes."

He flashed his teeth at me, smiling for the first time, and grabbed the bottom of his shirt. As soon as it cleared his head, though, the smile was gone.

"I like your smile," I said, wrapping my arms around his waist, stopping him from reaching for his pants. "What will it take to get you to smile more?"

"You want me to show my teeth?"

"I want you to show your happiness. If smiling isn't how fey usually show it, then teach me how to see it. It's not easy to read your expressions."

He studied my face for a moment.

"Humans run when we smile."

"Ah. It's probably the sharp teeth."

"Yes."

"So you don't smile because you don't want to scare people off?"

"Yes."

"Well, I'm not about to run away scared. It took too much work to get that ring on you. Smile away, Solin. I'm not going anywhere."

He grinned at me and lowered his lips to mine in a tender kiss that lasted for three seconds before he showed me what he was really feeling. His passion and need stole my breath and set my world spinning. When he finally tore his mouth from mine, I was dizzy and panting for air.

He picked me up and carried me back to the bed. I petted his chest as he gently eased me back then shifted my hold to play with his ears as he trailed kisses down my throat.

"You're still wearing too many clothes," I said when he started going lower. I was all for oral, but I wanted more this time. I wanted all of him.

He stood up and quickly removed his pants. My gaze drifted down his torso to his hard length and muscled thighs. I licked my lips, remembering what it'd been like to go down on him. Torn, I wondered which I wanted more. To teach him what sixty-nine meant or to finally have him inside me.

He reached down and stroked himself, deciding me.

"I love when you do that," I said, getting to my knees.

He continued his unhurried movements as I skated my fingers up his legs and leaned in for a lick.

"You were really quiet the last time I did this," I said. "It's hard to know what you like when you're quiet."

"I like all of it."

I gently removed his hold and placed his hand on the back of my head.

"Then show me," I said.

With a smile, I opened my mouth and wet his length before taking him as deep as I could manage. His fingers curled into my hair. I moaned my approval and withdrew enough to swallow before gliding down his length again. This time, there was more pressure on the back of my head.

I caught his other hand and placed it by the first as I continued to work his cock with my mouth. He made a pained sound and gave the barest thrust when I bobbed down. With my hands braced on his thighs, and I increased the pace. He groaned.

"Brooke." The single word sounded equal parts torment and adoration.

Sliding my hands around to grab his ass, I opened my throat and tried to go all the way. He was so big and the fit so tight that it burned a little. He hissed out a breath and ran his hand over the back of my head as I gave up and withdrew to his crown.

Tilting my head to meet his lust-filled gaze, I bobbed partway down his length before returning. He stroked my cheek and smoothed my hair back. I loved that he kept touching me with one hand while guiding my movements with the other. The gentle pressure he used to help me set the pace set me on fire because he had the strength to be aggressive but chose not to use it.

With a lick, I eased away and sat back on my knees.

"I like doing that. When you use your hands to guide me, it turns me on even more, which is making it really hard to choose. Do you want me to keep doing that, or do you want to lie down with me?"

He didn't hesitate to nudge me onto my back and join me on the mattress. He kissed me again, stealing my breath as his weight settled over me. I wrapped my legs around his waist, more than ready to consummate our commitment to each other. He nibbled along my jaw and down my throat before returning to my mouth. When he did, I felt the press of his crown at my opening. I arched, sinking onto him by an inch.

"Hold still, Brooke," he rasped.

"No way. You're taking too long."

"I don't want to hurt you."

"You won't."

He didn't listen. He continued to ease into me, inch by inch. And I was glad for it because even after two orgasms, it was still a snug fit that might have hurt if he'd rushed things.

But it was bliss once he was fully seated and rocking into me. I gripped his shoulders as he found a rhythm we both liked. He reached between us and palmed my breast. My core clenched around him. He grunted, and the pace briefly faltered before speeding up.

"Yes," I whispered. "Just like that."

He was hitting that sweet spot inside of me again and again. Everything started to tighten. I could feel my release building, climbing higher and higher.

With a brutal thrust, he shattered my control. The orgasm ripped through me, tearing from my throat in another keening cry that ricocheted off the walls. I clenched hard around him, and he didn't stop thrusting as the intense pleasure rolled through me in waves of endless bliss.

His rhythm faltered, and he came with a roar that shook the windows. Each twitching pulse of his cock washed my insides with heat and triggered pleasant aftershocks. His movements slowed but didn't stop completely until he'd emptied himself.

He kissed me hard and set his forehead to mine.

"Are you tired or hungry?" he asked.

"No. Just really, really happy."

"Good," he said, starting to move within me once more.

My eyes went wide.

"Again?" I asked.

"Again."

CHAPTER THIRTEEN

My legs shook with each step.

"Please, Brooke. Let me carry you," Solin begged as he walked backward down the stairs in front of me.

"Nope. Vertical movement is good for me." Clothes were good for me too, but all he'd allowed me was his shirt, which was thankfully long enough to cover my bare ass. I was sure Sophia would appreciate my effort and his grudging generosity.

"It's stretching out my sore muscles. And because I'm so sore, I think I'm going to need a long, hot bath after dinner too."

He flashed his teeth in a cringe, and I grinned.

"It'll be fun. I'll let you help."

He grunted and watched me until I made my way to the first floor. The sun had set hours ago, and my stomach wouldn't stop growling. However, Sophia and dinner were missing.

Shuffling to the kitchen, I found a note on the counter.

Based on all the yeses I heard, I'm guessing congratulations are in order. I've heard through the rumor mill that the first few days are the roughest on the girl-parts, so I packed a bag and

am staying at Mom and Dad's house for a bit. Stop by and say
hi whenever you're up for it.
Sophia

"What does it say?" Solin asked.

"Sophia went to stay with Mom and Dad. She doesn't mean her parents, does she?" I could count on one hand the number of families who'd made it through the initial earthquakes intact.

"No. Mom and Dad are Mya and Ryan's parents. They belong to all of us."

"Okay. Well, I guess that means I'm making dinner," I said, looking around. Honestly, I didn't want to cook. I wanted to sit in a warm tub and give my vagina a well-deserved break.

Solin, the beautiful man, seemed to read my disappointment because he reached into the cupboard and pulled out a box of snack cakes.

"You eat this and tell me how to make your favorite dinner." Without waiting for my agreement, he picked me up and sat me on the cold quartz counter. It was heaven. I'd worry about sanitizing later.

I ate a snack cake and told Solin what to do. He listened to each instruction like I was telling him how to perform a surgery. His attentiveness and care over something so mundane just because he knew it was important to me made me love him even more. When he presented me with a plateful of the finished product, I kissed him hard.

"Thank you for caring about me enough to make dinner, Solin. Just for that, I'll lick and kiss this until you make the windows shake," I said, palming the erection he'd tucked into his pants to come downstairs.

Since the first time, it hadn't ever gotten soft. That couldn't be healthy. If not for him, then for me.

"I like when you lick and kiss. Hurry up and eat."

I laughed, shifted to a new spot on the counter, and took my time. He didn't seem to mind, though, as I playfully fed him bites of what he'd made.

"Do you like it?"

He grunted.

"It is not my favorite meal. You are."

I grinned and fed him another bite.

"Oh, I know I am. But if you eat too much of me today, you won't be able to have any tomorrow."

His expression grew troubled.

"Ghua told me too much pussy licking could make you sore."

"You talked to someone about eating me out?"

"No. We talked about Eden, Ghua's female. He can only lick her four times a day now. He licked too much and broke his favorite part for three days."

"Oh boy. How many times a day was he licking her?"

Solin grew thoughtful.

"Too many?"

I snorted.

"How many times a day do you plan on licking me?"

"If I never stop, does it count as one?"

"Ha! Nope. Each time you make me come counts as one licking."

I didn't like the speculative look in his eyes.

"Wait. Each time I come or fifteen minutes. Whichever happens first counts as one."

He gave me a grumpy look, and I knew then that he really would keep me locked up in the house for days if I let him.

Setting my mostly eaten meal aside, I tugged him to stand between my legs.

"I don't want to deny you anything, but I'm human and fragile. Too much sex and licking makes me sore. That's why I told you I was hungry and want a bath. I loved everything we did, and I definitely want to do it again. But I need a break."

He grunted.

"Can I draw you while you rest in the bath?"

"Of course."

I WOKE with a stretch and smiled at the feel of a heavy arm circling my waist. Holding still, I listened to him breathe, the slow and steady rhythm telling me he still slept.

Last night's bath had been a revelation. While I soaked, we talked, and he drew me. I'd already known a fair amount about the fey. That they preferred meat over all other foods. Sometimes, the sunlight hurt their eyes and they needed to wear sunglasses. They were incredibly strong and our only defense against the hellhounds and the hordes of infected, who were growing increasingly smarter. There was also a rumor that sleeping with them passed their immunity from infection to their partner.

What I hadn't known was that Solin loved watching the moon. That he was dying to hold a newborn baby. That he was obsessed with my nose, of all things. That he hated the taste of snack cakes. That he seriously found the taste of me addictive. And that he doesn't need anywhere close to the same amount of sleep I do. That, or he was afraid I'd run. Because I'd woken up several times throughout the night and heard the faint scratch of pencil to paper.

Rolling in his arms, I smiled when he opened his eyes.

"Good morning, handsome. Did you get enough sleep?"

He grunted.

"Want to join me in the shower and maybe go for a walk after?"

"Yes."

He kissed my forehead, wrapped his arms around me, and stood with me. I squealed and held on tight.

"I will not drop you, my Brooke."

"I'm sure you won't." I laid my head against his bare chest and hoped no one was watching the windows and saw my bare ass.

Solin really liked me naked. It made it easier to touch me anywhere and everywhere. I let him wash me in the shower. He played with my breasts for a long time but was brief and gentle between my legs. I returned his consideration by taking my time to soap his still hard length until he came with a groan. We brushed our teeth together. He stole my towel and made me walk in front of him to the bedroom.

"So, what do you like better? My boobs, my butt, or my legs."

"All of you."

"Cheater. Now are you going to tell me where you hid my clothes?"

He grinned at me.

"I can't see my favorite parts when you wear clothes."

"I'll make you a deal. I'll show you a new pose that I think you're going to really like in exchange for my clothes."

"Show me."

"Lie down on the bed." He quickly obliged.

I grabbed his sketch pad, which was open to a picture of me sleeping. My nipple was just peeking out from under my arm and the edge of the blanket. It looked sexy as hell and tempted me to flip back to see what else he'd drawn. But it also tempted me to give him something even hotter to sketch.

"You'll need these," I said, handing the pad and pencil to him.

Straddling his hips, I lowered myself, and I grabbed his length. His avid gaze flicked between my face and where our bodies almost met.

"Are you sore?" he asked.

I smiled.

"Only a little. Are you ready to draw what you see?"

"Yes."

I sank deeper, feeding his cock into my opening. I took my time, moving slowly until I was fully seated and aching.

"Now watch," I said, leaning back to brace myself on his thighs before rotating my hips.

He made a pained sound, his gaze locked on where he slid in and out of me.

"Does it hurt?" I asked.

"No."

"Good."

Balancing on one hand, I closed my eyes and used the other to toy with my clit. The faint scratch of pencil on paper brought a knowing smile to my lips. I used every move I had to make him forget what he was doing, all the while bringing myself closer to completion.

The sound of the pad hitting the floor was the only warning I had before his hands grabbed my hips and he took control. I lasted a second after that. He was right behind me.

Panting, I collapsed onto his chest.

"Did I hurt you?" he asked.

"No. That was so good."

I felt him twitch inside of me.

"Hold that thought until after our walk."

He grinned at me but didn't stop me from getting up and closing myself in the bathroom. When I was done, he had my clothes waiting for me. I dressed and went downstairs to find him with his sketch pad in hand, waiting by the door.

"I should probably head back to Tenacity and let them know I'm moving out. I don't have a lot, but what I have, I'd rather not leave behind."

"I will take you," he promised.

"Do you maybe want to leave that here?" I asked.

"No. I promised Shax that I would show him what a sketch is."

"Wait...what pictures are you going to show him?"

"All of them."

I took the pad from him and thumbed through the pages. He'd created his own porn magazine, all pictures but no words, thanks to me.

"Are you okay with all your friends—"

"Brothers."

"Brothers seeing me naked? Like, I could take all my clothes off and walk around in front of them, and you'd be okay with that?"

He blinked at me, thinking it over, then looked down at the last picture he'd done of me riding him. He'd drawn my pussy eating his cock with epic detail. If it had been just that, I would have been okay with it. But he'd drawn all of me as well in perspective. So our genitals were up close and personal to the viewer, with my head tipped back and smaller.

"I'm fine with you showing some of the drawings." I flipped through the pages. "But not all of them, okay? They don't need to know what *my* bits look like, do they?"

"No."

"Here," I said, carefully tearing out the one of me sleeping. "Take this one with you. It's tastefully done and beautiful. You should be proud of it."

He folded it up and tucked it into his pocket.

"Now, let's go tell the world I put a ring on it. I want everyone to know you're mine and I'm never letting go."

He drew me into his arms and kissed my forehead.

"Good. Pictures aren't enough. I want to you to stay forever."

My heart melted, and I knew even the end of the world wouldn't be able to pull me away from Solin. He was perfect and all mine.

EPILOGUE

A FEW DAYS LATER...

SOLIN LEFT the table to answer the knock at the door.

"Are you sure about this?" I asked, continuing my conversation with Sophia. "There's no reason for you to leave. Matt had us packed in the Tenacity houses like we were sardines. There's more than enough room in here for three people. Plus, you like to cook."

She laughed.

"I promise to stop by with meals until you tell me to quit it. But I really want to do this. I enjoyed living with Solin, and I'm so happy for you two. I'm still hoping I'll connect with someone, you know?"

I heaved a sigh and nodded, knowing I couldn't begrudge her what I'd found with Solin.

"Do you know who it'll be?" I asked.

"Angel is here," Solin said, interrupting our conversation as he returned to the kitchen with a pregnant, blonde woman in tow.

The way he kept glancing back at her, his gaze flicking to her face then her belly, had me grinning.

"He's dying to cop a feel," I said. "Babies are his life goal."

Angel smiled.

"You must be Brooke. Mind if I sit?"

"Not at all."

She glanced at Solin as she took the chair at the end of the table.

"You're welcome to give my belly a feel, but the baby's not moving right now."

He went to the cupboard and pulled out a snack cake. She shook her head and ran a hand over her stomach.

"I'm going to be so fat," she said. "They've caught on to the fact that the baby kicks when I eat."

"Just another perk to being pregnant," I said.

"Another?"

"I'm betting you get whatever you want when you want it. Back rubs. Food. A ride."

"Ha! It's a double-edged perk sword. I have to fight for the right to use my own two feet. And there's a lineup for who gets to be in the room for the delivery. My baby dispenser is going to be well-viewed come birthing time."

She reached into her bra and withdrew a piece of paper.

"Speaking of well-viewed baby dispensers, I was wondering if you knew about this."

The unfolded drawing she set on the table made my eyes go wide. While I stared, she accepted the snack cake from Solin and started eating as if she hadn't just set down an up-close, rudimentary drawing of a vagina.

I looked at Solin, who was already squatted down beside Angel with his head cocked as he stared at her stomach.

"Who drew this?" I asked. Because I knew it hadn't been Solin. He was way too skilled for a circle surrounded by two lines with a bunch of squiggles.

"Turik," Solin said. "I was teaching him how to sketch. He wanted to draw a pussy. I described it to him, but he does not sketch well."

"And that's why I'm now getting requests for art classes and human models. Emily is having a hard time getting women to volunteer for dinner dates, and I'm struggling to get any gender to volunteer for massages. Do you know how impossible it would be to get a girl to say yes to posing nude so a bunch of fey can stare at her?"

"Brooke poses."

Sophia busted out laughing while Angel and I stared at Solin.

"Babe, are you saying you want me to pose for your brothers? That means they get to stare at my boobs and think all the things you think when you're staring at my boobs."

He frowned and opened his mouth to say something, but Angel interrupted.

"He's kicking. Grope away, Solin."

Solin didn't just put his hands on her. He leaned in and set his ear on her belly while his hand roamed the surface. The absolute wonder in his expression had me loving him even more.

"Nice ring," Angel said, looking down at his hand.

"It means I am Brooke's," he said absently.

She smirked at me.

"What you teach one of them, you teach all of them, whether you want to or not. They suck at keeping secrets."

"I'm sorry about the drawing. Maybe instead of asking for women to pose, a fey would be willing to volunteer. You know, like those wine and paint night things that used to be a thing. We could get a group of six girls together, give them a drink, feed them some snacks, then let them stare at what they're missing out on. Granted, the fey wouldn't get to see any naked humans, but they'd still be the center of attention."

Angel gave me a speculative look.

"That might be just what Tenacity needs. More dicks hanging around." She sniggered. "Would you be willing to teach it?"

"Sure. Solin found a ton of supplies."

"This is good. Really good. Hopefully, it'll be another way to remove the bias the women have against the fey."

Angel finished her last bite of the snack cake but didn't move to shoo him away. It'd be like kicking a puppy if she did. He was so damn happy listening to her baby.

"I think he needs one of his own," Angel said, noting the direction of my gaze.

"The way we're going, he'll get one."

He lifted his head from Angel's stomach to look at me, a hungry light in his eyes.

"Nope. We're on a room break, remember? I still have another hour and a half."

Angel laughed and stood now that she was free.

"You sound like Eden. She swears Ghua would keep her locked in the house if she didn't put a limit on the number of times they could have sex a day. I think she finally got him down to four."

Solin made a pained sound, and I patted his arm.

"We're still in the honeymoon phase. Don't worry. We can double that for another week."

"And that's why I'm moving out," Sophia said.

"I heard about that," Angel said. "Emily is helping the fey who are interested, which is all of the unclaimed ones, put their names on paper for a lottery drawing."

"We wanted to give them all a fair chance," Sophia said with a smile.

"You are a nice woman, Sophia, but I am glad you chose not to love me," Solin said. "Brooke is better."

Sophia and Angel laughed as Solin came over and kissed the top of my head. I grinned and took his compliment for the adoration it was. He was so perfect for me.

I hoped whoever Sophia drew would be just as incredible.

AUTHOR'S NOTE

This side story started after I released Demon Disgrace when fans of these adorable dark fey realized they'd need to go a whole year before the next book. I wanted to give something back to the readers who've been waiting so patiently for their answers and Molev's return. The idea was to create a story that was independent enough to be read away from the series. That meant lighter on the world building and plot and heavier on the romance. After brainstorming a few ideas with my author friends, the idea of a young artist, Brooke, looking for the fey of her dreams was born.

The challenge was to fit it into my writing schedule without pushing back any release dates (no one wanted that!). The solution was writing it slower but posting a chapter a week in my reader group. Based on the comments, they loved it!

Since not everyone is into Facebook, I've made this available in other formats as well. Newsletter subscribers were notified that they could/can download it for free via the book-extras link on my website. For those reluctant to exchange their email address for some free reading material, the book can also be purchased for a nominal cost via retailer sites. This option was made available for any reader who wants to support the growth of this series. All proceeds from this book will used to bring the next book in the Resurrection series to audio (it's a cost prohibitive endeavor).

Whatever method you chose, I hope you enjoyed this additional glimpse into the Resurrection world. I have a few more ideas if this one resonates well!

Be sure to subscribe for my newsletter via my website mjhaag.melissahaag.com/subscribe so you keep up on all my writing news. I only send monthly, so I won't spam your inbox.

Until next time, happy reading!
Melissa

THE
RESURRECTION
CHRONICLES

Humor, romance, and sexy dark fey!

BOOK 1: DEMON EMBER

In a world going to hell, Mya must learn to accept help from her new-found demon protector in order to find her family as a zombie-like plague spreads.

BOOK 2: DEMON FLAMES

As hellhounds continue to roam and the zombie plague spreads, Drav leads Mya to the source of her troubles—Ernisi, an underground Atlantis and Drav's home. There Mya learns that the shadowy demons, who've helped devastate her world, are not what they seem.

BOOK 3: DEMON ASH

While in Ernisi, cites were been bombed and burned in an attempt to stop the plague. Now, Marauders, hellhounds, and the infected are doing their best to destroy what's left of the world. It's up to Mya and Drav to save it.

BOOK 4: DEMON ESCAPE

While running from zombies, hellhounds, and the people who kept her prisoner, Eden encounters a new creature. He claims he only wants to protect her. Eden must decide who the real devils are between man and demon, and choosing wrong could cost her life.

BOOK 5: DEMON DECEPTION

Grieving from the loss of her husband and youngest child, Cassie lives in fear of losing her remaining daughter. To gain protection, Cassie knows she needs to sleep with one of the dark fey and give him the one thing she isn't sure she can. Her heart.

THE
RESURRECTION CHRONICLES

The apocalyptic adventure continues!

BOOK 6: DEMON NIGHT

Angel's growing weaker by the day and needs help. In exchange for food, she agrees to give Shax advice regarding how to win over Hannah. If Angel can help make that happen, just maybe she won't be kicked out when her fellow survivors find out she's pregnant.

BOOK 7: DEMON DAWN

In a post-apocalyptic world, Benna is faced with the choice of trading her body and heart to the dark fey in order to survive the infected.

BOOK 8: DEMON DISGRACE

Hannah is drinking away her life to stanch the bleeding pain from past trauma. Merdon, a dark fey with a violent history, relentlessly sets out to show her there's something worth living for.

BOOK 9: DEMON FALL

June never planned to fall in love. She had her eyes on the prize: a career and independence. Too bad the world ended and stole those options from her. Maybe falling in love had been the better choice after all.

THE BEASTLY TALES

Beauty and the Beast with seductively dark twists!

BOOK 1: DEPRAVITY

When impoverished, beautiful Benella is locked inside the dark and magical estate of the beast, she must bargain for her freedom if she wants to see her family again.

BOOK 2: DECEIT

Safely hidden within the estate's enchanted walls, Benella no longer has time to fear her tormentors. She's too preoccupied trying to determine what makes the beast so beastly. In order to gain her freedom, she must find a way to break the curse, but first, she must help him become a better man while protecting her heart.

BOOK 3: DEVASTATION

Abused and rejected, Benella strives to regain a purpose for her life, and finds herself returning to the last place she ever wanted to see. She must learn when it is right to forgive and when it is time to move on.

Becareful what you wish for...

Prequel: Disowned

In a world where the measure of a person rarely goes beneath the surface, Margaret Thoning refuses to play by its rules. She walks away from everything she's ever known to risk her heart and her life for the people who matter most.

Book 1: Defiant

When the sudden death of Eloise's mother points to forbidden magic, Eloise's life quickly goes from fairy tale to nightmare. Kaven, the prince's manservant, is Eloise's prime suspect. However, when dark magic is used, nothing is as simple as it seems.

Book 2: Disdain

Cursed to silence, Eloise is locked in the tattered remains of her once charming life. The smoldering spark of her anger burns for answers and revenge. However, games of magic can have dire consequences.

Book 3: Damnation

With the reason behind her mother's death revealed, Eloise must prevent her stepsisters from marrying the prince and exact her revenge. However, a secret of the royal court strikes a blow to her plans. Betrayed, Eloise will question how far she's willing to go for revenge.